W9-DCV-765

Her attacker was back.

Panic sent her pulse racing. Flashlight in hand, she ran to the attic steps, taking the offensive. She wouldn't be a victim again.

"Don't move," she shouted.

But it wasn't her attacker coming up the steps. Chief Winters came toward her. She should take a step back but she couldn't move. Something about him had her heart fluttering. He lifted her chin with his finger.

She wanted to tell him what a romantic cliché his action was, but then she'd be admitting her attraction. And she couldn't admit that. She'd never risk her heart again. Even if she were willing, something stood between them.

"What are you doing up here again?" he asked her.

She couldn't tell anyone what she'd done, especially not him. "Chief..."

"Jewel, don't you think it's about time you call me Colin?"

His voice was so gentle, she could almost forget he was here on official business. But that would be a mistake.

"Colin, I—"

But she never got a chance to speak. A scream tore through the attic.

Elizabeth Goddard is an award-winning author of more than twenty novels, including the romantic mystery *The Camera Never Lies*—winner of a prestigious Carol Award in 2011. After acquiring her computer science degree, she worked at a software firm before eventually retiring to raise her four children and become a professional writer. In addition to writing, she homeschools her children and serves with her husband in ministry.

Books by Elizabeth Goddard

Love Inspired Suspense

Mountain Cove

Buried
Untraceable
Backfire
Submerged
Tailspin
Deception

Freezing Point
Treacherous Skies
Riptide
Wilderness Peril

Visit the Author Profile page at Harlequin.com.

DECEPTION

ELIZABETH GODDARD

HARLEQUIN® LOVE INSPIRED® SUSPENSE

If you purchased this book without a cover you should be aware
that this book is stolen property. It was reported as "unsold and
destroyed" to the publisher, and neither the author nor the
publisher has received any payment for this "stripped book."

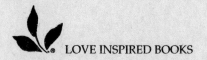

Recycling programs
for this product may
not exist in your area.

LOVE INSPIRED BOOKS

ISBN-13: 978-0-373-04404-7

Deception

Copyright © 2016 by Elizabeth Goddard

All rights reserved. Except for use in any review, the reproduction or utilization of
this work in whole or in part in any form by any electronic, mechanical or other
means, now known or hereinafter invented, including xerography, photocopying
and recording, or in any information storage or retrieval system, is forbidden without
the written permission of the editorial office, Love Inspired Books, 195 Broadway,
New York, NY 10007 U.S.A.

This is a work of fiction. Names, characters, places and incidents are either the
product of the author's imagination or are used fictitiously, and any resemblance to
actual persons, living or dead, business establishments, events or locales is entirely
coincidental.

This edition published by arrangement with Love Inspired Books.

® and TM are trademarks of Love Inspired Books, used under license. Trademarks
indicated with ® are registered in the United States Patent and Trademark Office,
the Canadian Intellectual Property Office and in other countries.

www.Harlequin.com

Printed in U.S.A.

As far as the east is from the west,
so far has He removed our transgressions from us.
–Psalms 103:12

Dedicated to my Lord and Savior, Jesus Christ
who paid my ransom.

Acknowledgments

My heartfelt thanks and gratitude goes out to all those who support my writing endeavors. First I thank my family, of course—my husband and boys who put up with my frequent forays into other worlds without them. We've been eating a lot of pizza and fast food lately, I know, but hey, don't you love it when Mom gets that book money? I also want to thank my dear writing buddies, you know who you are, and my new writing friends—I couldn't do this without your encouragement and support. And as always, thanks to my amazing editor, Elizabeth Mazer, for her insights into making my manuscripts the best they can be. Last and never least, I appreciate the encouragement from my agent, Steve Laube. Signing me as a client (has it already been over five years?) was a huge validation to me as a writer. Thanks, Steve!

ONE

Dead Man Falls
Mountain Cove, Alaska

Edging closer to the precipice that over-looked the plunging waterfall, Jewel Caraway risked a glance down. Vertigo hit. Dizziness mingled with worry.

Meral and Buck should have beaten Jewel to the falls where they had planned to meet up.

"Meral!" she yelled.

The roar of the water that cascaded hun-dreds of feet below drowned out her calls, sucking them down with the rushing water. A foaming whirlpool twisted where the froth-ing, tumbling force pounded the pool at its base. Misty spray drifted up and enveloped Jewel in a sheen of moisture. The sound of her voice could never compete with the rumbling growl of the cataract.

She tugged out her cell phone before she remembered she would get no cell signal here. The only signal she ever had was in Mountain Cove proper. She put the cell away, her gaze drawn back to the waterfall.

Powerful and dangerous.

Beautiful and terrifying.

Dead Man Falls was a force to be reckoned with. That was if one were to take the plunge and get sucked into the swirling torrent at the base.

Kayakers had attempted to navigate the drop and failed.

Part of a rainbow, transparent and fading into the mist, caught her attention. Mesmerized, Jewel stood at the edge of the rocky, moss-covered ledge that was flanked by spruce and hemlock, firs and cedars in the lush, temperate rainforest. She watched the churning at the bottom of an endless vortex that would trap anyone or anything unfortunate enough to fall. She wondered what secrets it held in its depths—then flinched at the memory of how she had buried a secret of her own and never thought about it again. That was until Meral, the sister she hadn't seen since Jewel had eloped twenty years ago, had arrived on her doorstep with her new husband.

And now they were both missing.

"Meral!" she called again. "Buck!"

Uncertainty roiled inside, tumultuous like the falls.

Those two had gotten lost somehow, which seemed impossible. They'd been hiking together when Jewel realized she'd forgotten her water and had needed to go back. They had gone on ahead of her on the well-defined trail, and the plan had been they would stop at the falls and wait until Jewel could catch up. Where could they have gone?

A twig snapped. Before she could turn,

a blunt object smashed into her back. Pain erupted along with her scream as the force of the blow propelled her forward.

Airborne, Jewel plummeted through the clouds and mist, feeling as if her stomach had been left behind on the cliff's edge.

Terror was catching up with her.

The spray of the waterfall engulfed her. At the last possible moment, she dragged in a breath and fell into the jaws of the beast she'd admired with a healthy fear only moments before. The wrath of the whirlpool plunged her deeper, twisting and tossing, bashing her against sunken boulders.

Dizziness and nausea held her captive within the vortex. The pounding water pushed her deeper, then turned her over again in the same way a crocodile rolled its meal to make it tender.

I'm not ready to die!

Lungs burning, Jewel shoved down the fear. The most important thing she'd learned from self-defense classes with local police chief

Colin Winters was not to panic. The violent water was nothing more than an assailant bent on harming her. She could only escape by slipping out of its grip. On the fringe of consciousness, Jewel did a flutter kick, swimming with all her might, and forced her body down and deep below the backwash.

Then she felt it.

The smooth water.

She'd escaped!

Disoriented, unable to tell which way she should go, she allowed the current to sweep her downstream and away from the falls. Jewel opened her eyes and fought through her exhaustion to try to swim toward the surface.

I can do this.

But fear and doubt clawed at her, threatening to drag her down and keep her under. Her lungs burned and screamed as she fought her way to the surface. And in that moment, the instance before she breached, she saw rocks and trees blurred at the top of the ledge from which she'd fallen…along with a figure. A *human* figure.

She'd thought, she'd hoped, that a branch had fallen from a tree and somehow shoved her in the back, sending her over to plummet into the river.

The way the figure stood there, the wide, deliberate stance, she knew…she *knew* that he or she had pushed Jewel. Intentionally shoved her into Dead Man Falls to what should have been her death. And she hadn't made it to safety yet. She could still die today in this river.

Why? Why had she been pushed?

The figure disappeared in the thick canopy even as the current dragged Jewel away.

Finally breaching the surface, she pulled in a breath and braced herself for a new battle to survive the river with its multiple tiered rapids and falls.

Jewel couldn't be sure how long the river had taken her captive. How long she'd allowed herself to be carried away, floating on her back in order to save her energy for that moment, that one moment, when she might have a chance to escape. Except her reserves were almost depleted.

That moment hadn't come.

How much longer could she keep her head above the rushing torrent?

Her limbs grew tired and numb, even with her effort to conserve energy. She searched the bank for calmer waters to swim toward. A branch to grab. Anything.

She needed out of the water before she hit the rapids and another set of falls.

God, help me!

Just ahead she spotted the trunk of a dead tree, branches sprawling and reaching. This was her chance and likely her last one before the rapids. Before she drowned.

Jewel reached, but the current, ripping and swirling as the rapids approached, twisted her away. She had no control over her own body. Her own life. She wouldn't be able to grab the trunk.

Jewel was going to die. Despair engulfed her.

Excruciating pain stabbed across her shoulder and back. Her body suddenly jerked and her forward momentum stopped. Something had caught her. Wrenched her from the river's grasp.

Stunned, recoiling in pain, Jewel twisted around. A branch from the fallen trunk had snagged and cut her deeply, but had saved her life even as it had wounded her. She held on with everything in her.

This was the chance she'd been hoping for. She wouldn't lose it. After coughing up more water, she dragged in air and allowed a measure of relief to set in. Now to pass the next test.

This was no time to rest. She had to get out of the river.

She gripped the slick trunk and pulled herself up, higher out of the water until only her legs were beneath the surface. Slowly, she inched toward the bank.

Her left hand slipped, and she let out a cry as she slid deeper into the water. But she reached again, grappling with another branch to keep from slipping completely back into the river's grasp. If only she weren't already so weak from her injuries and exhaustion.

Finally, she reached the rocky outcropping of boulders hugging the bank and pulled herself out of the river completely. Laying flat across a slick boulder, Jewel rested her gaze on the swift river and its endless push toward the deeper waters of the channel.

I made it out. Thank You, Lord.

Jewel rallied and pushed to her knees to climb over more boulders. Every ache, every bruise, every scratch and sprain screamed in agony as the numbing power of cold water that had served as an anesthetic now seeped away.

Free of the rocky edge, Jewel crawled until the river was no longer a threat and fell face forward into the mossy loam. She clung to the dirt, breathed in the earth. She'd made it this far, and she would be grateful for small things.

She wouldn't think about getting out of the wilderness. Maybe by now Meral and Buck would have reported her missing.

How long would they wait until they called for help? How long would it take that help to find her?

Terror snaked over and around her like a living, deadly vine and squeezed. It would crush the life out of her if she let it. She shoved her growing fear down and focused on surviving. She'd escaped the river and would draw confidence from that.

But it wasn't just nature she had to contend with. Another danger loomed out there some-where. Someone had pushed her into the falls. They could still be out there.

Had they watched the river carry her away? Were they tracking her now, on the verge of approaching to finish her off?

The pain in her back throbbed in rhythm

with her innumerable other injuries. If the person who'd tried to kill her found her here now, nearly incapacitated after fighting and surviving Dead Man Falls and the river, Jewel wasn't sure her self-defense classes would do her a bit of good.

But she held on to the hope they believed she had drowned in the falls as per their intent.

Since Tracy—her friend and previous employee at Jewel's Bed and Breakfast—had dealt with a vicious stalker about two years ago, a visceral fear had taken over Jewel, a dread that followed her everywhere with the awareness of just how easily danger could get close. It had taken them all far too long to realize that the stalker, who had hidden his appearance from Tracy, had actually been staying as a guest at the B and B.

Jewel had taken the self-defense classes, hoping to instill confidence in her ability to protect herself and to push away fear. Yet now that fear twisted deeper, hooking her full and well.

If help didn't arrive soon, Jewel would have to spend the night here and rest before she could find her own way out. She crawled forward and into the brush to hide, hoping it would be enough camouflage if the person who'd tried to kill her came looking.

All Chief Colin Winters wanted to do was take the week off. The month. Or maybe even the whole year. What would it feel like not to answer a phone? Not to have an endless list of problems vying for his attention?

But when his cell rang and he spotted the fire chief's number, he answered.

"Winters." Something in David Warren's voice had Colin on edge.

"What is it?"

"It's Jewel Caraway."

Colin's heart seized up. He couldn't speak.

"She went into the river at Dead Falls Canyon."

As police chief, Colin was trained to push down the panic and act. But at this news he couldn't move, couldn't think. He pressed his hand against the wall for support. "Is she…"

"Someone called the state troopers, and we have an incident number. North Face Mountain Search and Rescue is on the scene, and I'm calling you. I knew you'd want to know immediately."

Colin heard the meaning behind David's words. David was aware that Colin thought Jewel was a special woman. They all did.

They hadn't found a body, but his relief was short-lived. Dead Man Falls deserved the name.

Colin had already exited his office and was making his way to the back door to get into his Jeep.

"We're meeting at the trailhead by the mouth of the river."

Sherry, the dispatcher, called after him. "Chief! Chief!" He ignored her.

"I'm on my way," he spoke into the phone.

When he plowed through the back door, a truck screeched to a stop in the parking lot.

"I figured you would be." David leaned out the open window.

Colin shoved his cell in his pocket and climbed in. He'd let the new fire chief drive. Though he was anxious to get to the river and be part of the search, his hands trembled. He wouldn't be any good at the wheel. Nor did he want David to see how he was struggling with this news. It hit him much too personally when he had no right.

David swerved out of the parking lot and onto Main Street, going over the speed limit, but Colin wasn't about to stop him. This was an emergency.

"You doing okay?" David glanced his way intermittently.

Colin barely nodded. "What happened? Do you know?"

"According to Tracy, she went hiking with her sister and brother-in-law. I don't know what happened or how she fell in."

"She's a skilled hiker. Knows what she's

doing." So how did this happen? He couldn't reconcile this with what he knew about her.

"I hope she's a better swimmer," David said.

Colin thought he would be sick. *God, please let her survive.*

But it seemed impossible.

Twenty aching minutes later, David parked his truck at the boat dock. Colin hopped onto the Warren family boat. Others from the North Face Mountain Search and Rescue team had already left for the scene. But David, who was on the team, too, had stayed behind, knowing Colin would want to be there.

"Thanks, David."

David started up the boat. "For what?"

"For waiting. For taking me there."

"Of course. You've saved my skin countless times. You were the one to figure out who had put Tracy in danger."

All part of the job. "Still, I appreciate it."

"I knew you'd want to help find Jewel."

The wind whipped over his face as the boat sped away from Mountain Cove. Colin stared ahead, going through all the possible scenarios in his mind, except the worst-case scenario. He couldn't think about finding Jewel's body.

The boat ride took far too long, and he was glad others had gotten to the trailhead and started the search before he and David arrived. Kayaks and other boats rested along the shore, all empty, all except one. Cade Warren—David's brother—stood on the deck hovering over maps. Colin followed David over to the boat and climbed aboard to speak to Cade, who was in charge of the search at the ICC, or Incident Command Center.

"Anything?"

"Nothing yet."

"Tracy's here with Solomon," Cade said. "You knew that, right?"

David straightened. Grinned at his brother.

"I wouldn't have it any other way. Jewel means the world to Tracy. Solomon'll find her."

Colin wasn't surprised to hear the news. David's wife, Tracy, was trained at search and rescue, as was her dog, Solomon. Plus, she used to work for Jewel at the B and B until the twins came along, and had a close relationship with her employer. It made sense that she'd rush out to help as soon as she learned what had happened.

"Where are they?" Colin asked.

Cade pointed at the map. "Sent them off here to search the riverbank. Later, we'll be looking…"

When Cade glanced up at Colin, he let his sentence trail off. He was glad Cade decided not to finish. He didn't want to think about dredging the river or this channel for a body. He was glad he wasn't in charge of the search.

Hopping off the boat and onto the small deck, he left David and Cade behind.

"Winters! Where are you going?"

"What do you think? I'm going to look for Jewel." He marched up the trail.

He didn't have time for pleasant conversation.

"Hold up." David left Cade behind to follow and jogged up to him.

Colin didn't wait for him, hiking up a few yards, then veering off into the forest to the left toward the river. That raging, deadly river.

David gripped his arm. "We'll find her, Winters. Though I have to say," he added with a frown, "I didn't realize you were in this deep."

"What are you talking about?"

Tracy rushed up to her husband. Breathless, she pointed. "I think Solomon's found something."

Colin and David followed Tracy through the woods, around trees and fallen trunks, over rocks and boulders to Solomon's bark and whine. Colin tensed at the dog's signals.

He knew Solomon had finally gotten certified as a cadaver dog.

He braced himself, unsure what they would find—a living, breathing Jewel or her body.

TWO

Something wet slid across her nose, eyes and mouth. Jewel stirred and tried to turn over to defend herself, but a bone-piercing throb coursed through her wrist.

A dog's whimper and continued licking steadied her breathing. Calmed her fear. She recognized the animal.

"Solomon." Her voice didn't sound like her own.

Footsteps, twigs snapping and breaking, resounded through the undergrowth on the river's edge.

"Jewel," Tracy said. "Are you all right?"

Relief swelled inside. "Depends on your definition."

Tracy spoke to someone nearby and then radioed others that Jewel had been found.

"Shouldn't you be home with your babies? Your twins?" Jewel managed.

"Grandma Katy needs her time with them. Besides, you had to know I would come looking for you. Solomon and I."

"Jewel!" A familiar, masculine voice joined Tracy's.

Jewel heard the immeasurable relief in his tone. That ignited her heart. She was alive. She had survived.

"Chief Winters," she croaked. *Colin.* She had always called him by his official title to keep personal feelings out of it. To keep her distance. Otherwise, the man could undo her resolve to protect her heart.

Her bruises throbbed with any movement or effort on her part. She squeezed her eyes shut, unwilling to look at him.

"We're here now, Jewel. You're going to be okay. You just rest now."

As other SAR members arrived and focused in on Jewel, they crowded him out and away.

"No! No... Chief Winters." She reached for him.

He stepped forward, closer again.

"I'm here, Jewel. I never left." His electric blue eyes pierced hers, concern and relief spilling from them. "What is it? What do you need?"

"Someone pushed me into those falls."

Anger rose in his gaze and maybe a little disbelief. "Can you describe him?"

"No...I..."

Chief Winters grabbed her hand. "Whoever it was, we'll find him, Jewel. Don't you worry. You're in good hands now. I have to go and make sure nobody else gets hurt."

Then he slipped out of the way of her search and rescue friends. Jewel endured the poking and prodding and assessing and finally the hefting and assisting her back to civilization.

On the helicopter ride back to Mountain Cove, Jewel closed her eyes, wanting to forget what had happened, wanting to pretend it had simply been a bad dream. Wanting to wake up with a body free of pain and evidence of the nightmare. But she couldn't let go of the blurred image of the person she'd seen standing at the top of the falls.

There hadn't been room for Chief Winters on the helicopter, and maybe she was glad about that so she would have time to think about what she'd seen exactly before having to answer his questions. But he was probably searching for who could have done this. Making sure others were warned a crazy person was out there.

At the small Mountain Cove hospital clinic, Doc Harland attended to all her bruises and scrapes. He didn't like the look of the deep gash along her shoulder and back from the fallen tree trunk's branches, but she knew that though painful, that injury had saved her life.

That particular gash needed stitches. Her

sprained wrist was already wrapped. Doc assured her it would heal within a few days.

"Hold still, dear." Doc Harland had anesthetized the gash so she couldn't feel the needle pricks as he stitched her up. "You aren't afraid of needles now, are you?"

"I can't stop shaking. My body has a mind of its own. I'm sorry."

"No need to apologize. You've had a scare. We'll give you something to calm you if you like."

"No, thank you." Jewel needed to stay alert. Figure this out. "Are Tracy, Meral and Buck still out there in the waiting room?"

"Far as I know. You want me to send someone to check?"

"No."

"I've treated a lot of folks in my life, but never anyone who has gone into those falls and survived. What happened out there?"

"If it's all the same to you, Doc, I'd like to forget about it." Jewel stared at the sterile wall. She might want to forget, but she knew she couldn't.

"I want to run a few tests. Draw some blood. But not today—you've already been through enough. I want to see you back in a week to look at those stitches and your wrist. We'll get the blood then."

Was Doc wondering if she had some sort of medical condition that had caused her to fall?

"There. All done." Doc Harland flipped down her gown.

"Jewel?" Meral peeked through the door. "I brought you some dry clothes."

"Come on in," Doc Harland said. "I'll leave you to change."

Doc Harland nodded and left to give her privacy.

Meral set the clothes—a pair of jeans, teal T-shirt, light jacket, shoes, socks and undergarments—next to Jewel. "I'm so sorry, Jewel. If we'd just stuck together this would never have happened." She wiped at the remnants of tears on her cheeks.

She started to hug Jewel, but then acted as though she'd thought better of it. Jewel must look terribly beat up and bruised. Admittedly, a hug would hurt right now.

Meral, short for Emerald, was in her thirties and ten years younger than Jewel. She'd been a teenager when Jewel had run away to marry Silas. Beautiful as she was, she looked fragile and pale at the moment.

"Are you okay?" Jewel found herself asking.

"I'm feeling nauseous. Buck insists on taking me back now. Are you almost ready?"

"Sure, I just need to change."

"You need help with that?"

"No, you go on now. I'll be out in a minute."

Meral nodded and left Jewel. Poor thing. She probably didn't know how to take what had happened. Jewel wasn't sure she did either. It was hard to comprehend.

Jewel took far too long to get into her clothes. Every movement, every twist and bend of her body hurt. She risked a glimpse in the mirror over the sink.

Big mistake.

She didn't even recognize herself.

Someone knocked softly on the door. Meral had timed it just right. They were both ready to get home. But how could Jewel let her guests at the B and B see her like this?

"Come in."

The door opened and in stepped Chief Winters, standing tall and intimidating in his official tan police uniform.

Her pulse jumped.

Whether from being startled at seeing someone other than Meral, or if it was her reaction to Chief Winters himself, she wasn't sure.

Seeing him here, clearly concerned about her, brought her more pleasure than it should.

She reminded herself he wasn't here for personal reasons but to question her officially. But she wasn't sure she was ready. Everything that had happened was starting to blur together.

What had she really seen? Had she simply imagined the figure on the ledge?

Chief Winters stepped completely in and closed the door behind him. His electric blue eyes always saw everything, and now they flashed with a powerful emotion. Before she could define it, the emotion was shuttered away.

What was the man thinking?

Jewel averted her gaze. She didn't see the chief of police often outside the self-defense class. And in the class she tried not to think about how tall and rugged he was, or the confident air he had about him. He was in his late forties, the same age as her husband, Silas, would have been if he hadn't died a decade ago. Silas and Chief Winters had been friends, not close, but friendly enough that they were on a first-name basis. And he'd always been warm and friendly to her, as well, and somewhat protective after Silas had died. All the more reason to keep her distance.

Jewel hung her head for a moment, instinctively, hating for him to see her like this, but then she quickly lifted her chin and faced him. She couldn't let him see how he affected her. She was surprised to see that today something new burned behind his gaze, and it wasn't warm or friendly. It was downright terrifying.

"What are you doing here?" she asked.

"Checking up on you. You had to know I'd come. How are you, Jewel?"

"Did you find them? The person who pushed me?"

He shook his head. "Not yet. I know you're tired and hurt, and this isn't the best time, but I'm going to need you to think about what happened and tell me everything. Start from the beginning. Who pushed you into the falls?"

"I don't know."

Jewel wanted to scream. She wanted to cry, but she wouldn't do that in front of Chief Winters. She missed Silas—wished she had someone here to hold her. She wanted to feel strong arms around her. Someone to tell her everything was going to be all right. That someone hadn't just tried to kill her, and she was only imagining things. And in a moment of weakness like this, Colin Winters was the only man who could fulfill those needs.

But she couldn't let him in that deep.

She'd lived in Alaska long enough that she was well aware of how to take care of herself. She'd run her B and B near the edge of the wilderness for more years than she wanted to admit. She wouldn't give in to that weakness.

I know how to survive.

I can do this.

Chief Winters stared at her, waiting patiently. She'd always liked that about him. But how did she answer his question? What could she tell him that would make any sense?

Jewel moved to sit in the chair against the wall. Colin didn't rush her, giving her a moment to think on the details of what had happened.

Some days Colin hated his job, and today

was one of those days. He hated having to pry answers out of people—especially people he cared about personally.

"Accidents happen, Jewel. People fall where they shouldn't all the time, including in the shower, where some die every year." He hated himself for this, but he had to ask her. He had to be certain. "Are you sure someone pushed you?"

She stared at the floor. Was she thinking it through?

Seeing Jewel like this undid him. Unraveled him from the inside out.

Jewel Caraway was a beautiful woman. One of the most beautiful he'd ever seen, and that included on the inside, where it mattered most. She was beautiful like Katelyn—a woman he'd loved—had been. Had a quiet elegance and grace about her, and the most captivating hazel-green, gold-flecked eyes. Colin shouldn't be thinking about her in that way, but he couldn't stop himself. Had never been able to stop himself for as long as he'd known her.

Except today, circles darkened Jewel's eyes, and her usually shiny, ash-blond hair was askew. Her face was bruised in a way that turned his stomach into knots.

He was the police chief, but he was a man, too, and Jewel had caught his attention the first time he'd met her. She reflected light like a precious gem. Her parents must have known she would when they had named her. She carried herself with the confidence of experience, but she'd never looked a day over thirty to him, though she was in her mid to late forties just like Colin.

Then he remembered himself.

In a professional capacity he'd come to make sure she was all right. But his true interest in her went deeper, even though he'd never let himself act on it. Her husband had been a friend, and Colin had never let his mind or heart stray before. Nor would that happen now, even though she was a widow.

In his eyes, she'd aged ten years in the past

few hours. Colin thought maybe he'd aged that much, too. Maybe more.

She could have died out there.

She pressed her face into her palms, her shoulders shaking. He'd never seen her undone like this, but it was understandable. Colin lost it then, too. He pressed his hand against her head, felt the softness of her hair. His heart thudded against his ribs.

"Please, Jewel. Talk to me."

She drew her face up, and her haggardness caught him afresh, sending a new pang through his chest.

"Meral, Buck and I had gone kayaking. They just got married and arrived two days ago. Were excited to be here and wanted to see southeast Alaska. She's my sister, and I haven't seen her in twenty years."

Jewel seemed to regret her last words, which came out rushed. An outburst to cover some deeper emotion hidden away? He'd let her tell him that story another time. Yet maybe there was something here that played a role in what had happened today.

"Go on," Colin said, nodding.

"We secured the kayaks in the bay and decided to hike up to the falls. We planned to be out for a few hours. A day at the most. I forgot my water and went back to get it. Buck and Meral went on ahead. I said I'd catch up to them. Meet them at the falls where the trail stopped. From there you could choose between two other trails, and I didn't want them to go farther without me. It shouldn't have been so complicated."

"And were they at the falls when you got there?"

"No. I stopped to watch the waterfall. Silas liked to explore waterfalls. Maybe you remember that we used to travel around to see the falls in the region, even as far south as Ketchikan. He liked to study them. Kayak over them, if possible."

"And what about you? Did you enjoy that, too?"

She shook her head. "I'm not into thrills."

No. He hadn't thought so. She was adventurous, yes, but was more the kind to enjoy the beauty rather than the challenge of nature.

"So did you call for Meral and… What is his full name again?" She'd only given her brother-in-law's first name when she'd mentioned him earlier. Colin didn't want to be too invasive. Let her tell the story. He hadn't met Buck yet. Apparently he'd just missed the man and Jewel's sister when he'd got to the clinic.

"Buck Cambridge. Yes, I called out for them when I made the falls, and they were not there. I heard a twig snap behind me. Before I turned, something slammed into my back."

Colin hated thinking about the bruises that covered the rest of her, if her face was any indication. "I'm just glad you survived. It seems…"

"Impossible. I know."

For a moment, Colin let himself visualize her battle, experience it with her. If he let himself think about it too long, he'd be visibly shaking, trembling like she was.

"Tell me the rest."

"After my initial panic, I swam beneath the backwash and let the current pull me away from the churning falls. I swam toward the surface to get air and happened to glance to the top of the falls."

"And what did you see?"

"Someone. Just a figure. My vision was blurred by water, but I saw someone for a split second before the water pulled me away."

"You sure it wasn't Meral you saw, arriving after you'd fallen in? She was the one to call this in. Her quick thinking got the search for you going."

Jewel closed her eyes. After a moment, she shook her head. "I don't think so. No, I'm sure it wasn't Meral. The jacket she's wearing is too bright—even though I couldn't make out the face of the person I saw, that color would have caught my eye. It was the person who pushed me in. They were standing exactly where I'd been before being pushed."

Colin hated that her story could be picked apart, especially since she appeared so frazzled. And after his experience in Texas, he resolved to look at the facts and only the facts. He couldn't go on gut feelings alone.

Jewel's experience and what she'd seen could be based entirely on her emotional state. But this was Jewel Caraway. Writing her off wasn't something he was willing to do. Colin would take her seriously. If someone truly had tried to kill her, then he would do everything he could to make sure she was safe.

He frowned. "Was the person you saw male or female?"

"I couldn't tell." She looked up at him again. "You do believe me, don't you?"

"Of course." He believed she wasn't deliberately lying, but could her memory be faulty? Eyewitness stories almost always conflicted. Everyone had his or her own perspective. Had Jewel really seen someone? And had that person pushed her?

"Did you see anyone else on the trail during your hike?"

"No."

"I'll need to question your sister and her husband." He wouldn't divvy this out to his officers. No. This investigation belonged to Colin.

"Of course. They're waiting out there. I'm surprised you didn't already meet and question them. They *are* still out there, aren't they?"

Colin let out a slow breath. Would she be disappointed if he told her they had already gone? A fact he found strange. What was more important to them than Jewel's well-being?

"Oh, wait. Meral wasn't feeling well." Disappointment edged her voice. "Maybe Buck wanted to get her home. Maybe they decided not to wait for me to get dressed."

Colin's throat tightened. Nice guy. "I'll

take you home, Jewel. Don't worry. Now can you think of any reason why someone would try to kill you?" Maybe this wasn't a random act, though he couldn't think of a single enemy she would have made. She was kind and generous, and her guests always raved about their experience at the B and B. But if he'd learned anything as a twenty-five-year police veteran, it was that everyone had dry bones buried in the backyard. As hard as it was to believe, Jewel would be no exception.

"I almost wish I did. Then it would be easy to find out who pushed me."

Colin agreed. "In that case, I don't want you to be alone until we figure this out. Do you understand?"

"That should be easy enough to comply with. After all, my sister is here now for a short visit."

Colin didn't bring up that she was supposed to be with her sister when someone had tried to kill her—Meral hadn't been any protection for her then. At any rate, maybe her sister and husband would stay until this investigation was closed. "Come on. I'll give you that ride home now. Doc give you some scripts?"

"Yeah, painkillers and an antibiotic, I think."

"Fine. I'll get you home first, then I'll run those over to the pharmacy for you."

Jewel stood, ready to leave, her confusion over the day's events evident, mingling with exhaustion from the strain on her beaten body. Colin was glad to be the one to see her safely home. If it was actually even safe. He'd determine that when he arrived.

He pursed his lips, envisioning what he wanted to do to her attacker or attackers once he got his hands on them, and before he put them in a jail cell. But that was all it was—a vain imagining.

He opened the door and assisted her out to the waiting room, where they found Tracy with David. Tracy said she had encouraged Meral to go back to the B and B, seeing that she wasn't feeling well, reassuring them that she and David would get Jewel home. Colin could see the relief in Jewel's eyes that she hadn't been abandoned, but all Colin could think was Tracy and David were behaving more like family to her than Meral and Buck. While Jewel thanked Tracy for finding her, Colin talked to David about going back to the falls to look around.

Then he ushered Jewel through the exit where his Jeep waited and assisted her into the passenger seat, taking care he didn't hurt her. On the drive back, he took the bumps and the potholes slowly and carefully.

Anger boiled beneath the surface at the thought of her injuries. At the thought of someone actually trying to hurt her. At the image of someone pushing her into those falls.

He would have to prevent them from trying again.

But he knew firsthand how difficult it could be to stop a killer. He'd attempted and failed before, and as a result, Katelyn, the woman he'd planned to propose to, had been murdered.

And he'd known all along who had wanted to kill her, and still Colin hadn't been able to prevent her murder. With no idea where to even look for Jewel's attacker, how was he going to be able to keep her alive?

THREE

The next morning, Colin walked the trail with one of his officers, Terry Stratford, along with Cade and David Warren, who were friends and had been part of the search and rescue for Jewel.

He almost wished Dead Falls Canyon, both the river and several waterfalls, were far from town, where they'd be less of a danger to the people under his jurisdiction, which included the city and borough of Mountain Cove and encompassed two thousand square miles, most of that wilderness in the Tongass National Forest.

But the majestic scenery and unparalleled adventures of the region were all part of the package. The splendor, the pristine nature and magnificent views brought tourists. One of the many reasons people chose to live here.

But beauty had turned deadly more than once.

After his officers and forest rangers had searched the area yesterday and came up empty-handed, he'd decided that Jewel's attacker was long gone, and there wasn't reason enough to close off the whole region to nature enthusiasts.

Today's revisiting of the crime scene hadn't turned up any evidence or clues either, so far. Jewel's party hadn't been the only one to hike the trails or view the falls, so there was no way to try to trace anyone's tracks.

Colin maintained a keen sense of his surroundings in case someone was watching him. He had that sensation as they hiked the trail, but it could simply be curious hikers wondering what had brought the police out on the trails today.

They'd walked the five-mile circular trail that led to the top where Jewel claimed to have stood and looked down. This was some of the most beautiful scenery in the world, and now it would likely be ruined for Jewel unless she could somehow put those events out of her mind.

He was asking for the impossible. Colin had moved to Mountain Cove to escape his own devastating experience in Texas. He hoped Jewel wouldn't have to take such drastic measures.

Under normal circumstances, he'd have his officers roam the woods now, searching again for evidence, rather than coming out here himself. He had enough paperwork stacked on his desk and phone calls to answer to last a lifetime, and the tourist season was only beginning.

But this wasn't normal. This was Jewel Caraway. The thought of losing her, that moment when he'd thought she could have been dead, had forced him to look deep, even though he knew he couldn't make it too personal and had to tread carefully.

As police chief, loving someone would only cloud his judgment and get someone killed one day—he'd already paid that price. He would never let that happen again. He found it easy to care about someone from a distance, but better not to care at all.

David and Cade stood next to him, staring down at the crushing force of rushing water. Listened to the roar. Felt the moisture cloud envelop them. No wonder she hadn't heard someone approach from behind until the instant before impact. And she certainly hadn't known to be wary of someone who would push her over.

"I'm still wondering how nature could push a body under and keep it there, and that body still survive," Cade said.

"Maybe it's more the nature of God that she survived." It was easy to believe that Jewel had a special place in God's heart like she had in Colin's.

"Why would someone try to kill her?" David asked. "Was it just a random act of violence?"

He voiced the question they were all wondering, but had no answer for yet. David had endured a fight to protect the woman he loved not long ago and understood better than most there had to be a reason. A secret not shared.

Finding the person responsible for the attacks against Tracy had taken far too long. Colin could still hear the questions from the city council echoing in his ears, and they mingled with the new questions. The same questions.

What are you going to do about it? How are you going to stop it before it happens again?

Two women approached the falls from the trail, pulling Colin from his thoughts. He nodded to David, Cade and Terry. They'd seen enough for now. They moved away from the falls and headed back down the trail.

"What do you know about her sister and brother-in-law?" Colin asked.

"Not much," David said. "They're newlyweds, I hear. I imagine it means a lot to Jewel that they've come to see her, since she's been estranged from her family for a long time.

Once when Silas and I were out fighting wildfires in the interior, he shared a little about Jewel. What a rare find she was."

Colin wouldn't argue with him there. Her name said it all.

"She comes from a wealthy family, and they didn't think Silas was good enough for her. When her parents made it clear they disapproved of him, he almost walked away. He loved her too much to tear her away, but in the end, he'd been selfish, after all. He couldn't let her go. They were young and impulsive."

"And that's why she hasn't been in touch with her family all these years?" Colin asked.

"They didn't give her much choice—her family disinherited her when she chose to marry him."

"What kind of parents did that? Disowned or disinherited their child?" Cade asked.

"That's just weird," Terry spoke as he led them down the trail.

Colin couldn't say much. Guilt and shame

over how he'd treated his own family had followed him here to Alaska. He'd left his parents behind in Texas and, as they aged, his sister was forced to take sole responsibility for their care. Colin hadn't been much of a son or a brother, but after what happened, he saw himself as a burden to his family—one they would be better off without. They must see what he wanted to forget every time they looked at him.

"She left it all behind—her family and the wealth—to follow Silas to Alaska." David kicked a rock down the path.

"I can see why he would think she was special," Colin said. "She must have loved the man deeply. It's not easy to live here or to give up your family. To give up wealth on top of that."

"You know, she could love deeply again, right?" David studied Colin.

Cade and Terry walked together up a ways. Colin was glad they hadn't heard David's question. He was just prying into Colin's personal thoughts. Either that or nudging him toward a place he had no business going.

They'd almost made the trailhead where they would kayak back to Mountain Cove, following the path Jewel's group had taken in their search. Colin eyed his friend. Understood the meaning behind his words.

"Jewel deserves someone far better than me." And if she had a wealthy family, she was more like Katelyn than he'd realized. That wealth had come between them more than once. Her wealthy family had questioned his investigation, blamed him for her murder as if he hadn't already been weighed down by it.

"So what do you think? Who do you believe is a suspect?"

"Hard to say at this point. The fact she has a wealthy family could be motivation for murder."

"But how if she's been disinherited?" David asked. "There has to be more to the story."

"There always is."

* * *

Meral had gone down to the kitchen to get Jewel a cup of green tea. Jewel was glad to have a minute of relative privacy. She was glad that she had people who cared about her enough to want to help her, but the hovering was already starting to feel overwhelming.

She definitely didn't like being confined to her room, even though her body was sore and she needed to recover from her injuries. Not to mention she had guests to attend to, but neither could she let any of them see her like this. She'd give it a day or two, leaving running the B and B to her staff, and hope it didn't take a week for her bruised body to heal. Jewel would give anything to forget about the fall and her injuries and to go back to life as usual. She needed normalcy. To get that, she would have to stop taking the painkillers. They made her groggy, and she couldn't think straight.

When she sat up, dizziness swept over her.

She made the mistake of glancing in the mirror over the dresser, and her mouth dried up.

Chief Winters saw me like this?

She shoved thoughts of what he must think of her out of her mind. His opinion shouldn't count. She couldn't care about that. After Silas's death, she almost hadn't survived the heartache. She'd given up her life and family to be with him, and now all she had left of that life were memories and heartache. The price of loving someone was too high.

She couldn't survive that pain again.

So for now she had to focus on other things until the unwelcome feelings in her heart went away.

One question nagged her. Why would someone want to kill her? Had it simply been random? Or had she been targeted? Jewel had no enemies that she knew about. No reason for someone to push her over.

Unless…

My secret.

Jewel pressed her hands over her heart.

God, please no. She needed the secret to remain dead and buried. She wasn't the same young woman who had made that mistake. Besides, no one knew about it, so no. That couldn't be it.

She was back to her question. And she didn't know why someone would try to kill her. When she was a child, her parents had taught her to be on her guard, not to trust easily, because there were too many people in the world who might try to hurt her or kidnap her because of their money. But it had been years since that had been an issue for her. No one in Alaska had even known she'd once been wealthy. Until Meral and Buck arrived a few days ago.

Now suddenly her life had been threatened. Could the two incidents be related?

And what of Meral's new husband, Buck? What did Meral really know about the man?

Jewel should be ecstatic that she had a second chance with the family she'd given up to come to Alaska. She thought she'd gotten over that hurt, too, until Meral. She wanted to be happy to see her sister, who had only been fifteen when Jewel had left. In fact, she had not known how much she'd missed her family.

But something was wrong. Very wrong. She should thank Buck Cambridge for bringing Meral—a wedding gift, he'd said. He'd found Meral's long-lost sister. But Jewel wasn't sure she really wanted to be found.

Something about Buck disturbed her. He didn't look at Meral the way Jewel's husband had looked at her when they'd fallen in love.

But who was Jewel to judge? How could she bring up her misgivings about Buck with Meral, a sister she barely knew? They were only just reconnecting. Getting to know each other again. It wasn't her place. She wouldn't do anything to destroy this chance at having her family again. If Jewel questioned her sister about Buck, then she would sound just like their parents had sounded when Jewel had fallen in love.

Those memories came rushing back, crushing the breath from her.

Jewel shoved from the bed. She wouldn't do that to Meral. She'd give her sister—a grown woman in her thirties, an experienced woman who had already been married before—the benefit of a doubt.

Jewel would let Chief Winters investigate and see what came of it without mentioning her suspicions about Buck.

She could trust Colin Winters. He was a good man and a good chief of police and had served Mountain Cove well. Maybe there were some in town who blamed him for the rise in the crime rate in recent years, accusing him of not being hard enough on suspects and criminals. Then others blamed him and his officers for using too much force. So much pressure from the community pushing him in different directions had to be brutal on him.

Jewel had never blamed him. People wanted to remove God from the equation of life and expect law and order to reign in His place.

Without God ruling people's lives, there was only chaos.

The words snagged at her heart, bringing to mind her own shortcomings. Her own hidden secret. She needed to check on it—see if it was still safe. Jewel peeked out the door into the hallway. All clear.

Jewel's bedroom was on the second floor. She tiptoed up another flight of stairs. Though unintelligible, Meral's voice could be heard, along with Katy Warren's, drifting up from the kitchen.

Katy was here? The grandmother and matriarch of the Warren clan was a dear friend, and Jewel wanted to go down and greet her, but now that she had a moment alone—something she might not get for a while—she needed to take a good long look at her past.

The one she'd buried, tucked away forever, safe and sound.

Creeping to the end of the hallway, she gently pulled down the stepladder to the attic. She climbed up into the hot and stuffy room.

She flicked on a light to add to the sunlight spilling through a dirty dormer window at the far end.

A raccoon had tried to nest up here, and Jewel had come up to chase it away on more than one occasion, but other than that, she hadn't been up here for months.

Dust motes and cobwebs had taken over the space. Jewel brushed away the webs as she moved. When Silas had bought the B and B, he had believed it would keep her occupied so she wouldn't worry about him traveling to fight wildfires. They'd hoped to turn the attic into an office or another room for a guest. Instead, it ended up serving as storage for old furniture and collectibles that Jewel planned to use to refresh the B and B decor, switching things out for seasons or special occasions.

And when he'd been away, she'd stored her more valuable collectible—if you could call it that—not just *in* the house but *with* the house.

If the house burned to the ground, her valuable would survive.

Jewel headed for the far corner, dreading what she was about to do. Acid churned in her stomach.

She moved a trunk, feeling an ache through her back and across her legs and arms. Maybe this wasn't such a good idea. She might accidentally tear the stitches and open up that nasty gash.

Plus, moving the trunk had made too much noise. She had to be quiet, or Katy and Meral would hear her movements.

Creak.

She froze. Her pulse jumped.

The sound had come from the attic. The rafters settling beneath the simple plywood flooring? Or something—someone—else?

At the falls she'd heard the snap of a twig right behind her. Shuddering, she slowly turned to look. See if someone was there, fearing what would happen if they were. She couldn't see the steps down into the hallway for the boxes and furniture stacked in her way.

Ever since Tracy's attacker had stayed in the B and B, Jewel had known she needed more protection than the rifles stored in a gun closet or a 9-millimeter semiautomatic pistol tucked away in her nightstand. She had needed to train in self-defense in case a day ever came when she would have to protect herself without the use of a firearm.

Granted, none of that had come in handy at the falls, except maybe to give her confidence to swim her way to freedom. Would she find herself using that training now? When she heard nothing more, she looked at the wall where the item was hidden behind a plank and reconsidered. Maybe she wasn't in the right frame of mind to revisit the past.

But there was only one reason Jewel could imagine someone would want her dead. She hadn't wanted to think about it, but as the walls of the attic closed in around her, she had to face the truth.

Another creak had her stiffening. Preparing for the worst.

"Who's there?"

How could anyone have come up here with her? She would have heard them, right? "Meral, is that you?"

Her knees shook. She was far weaker than she wanted to be. Too weak to deal with her secret right now. Jewel would come back another day. Maybe when Chief Winters returned from his look at the falls she would tell him everything.

Except he would be disappointed in her, and she didn't think she could bear that. She made her way through the maze of junk, heading for the steps out of the attic.

The sense of a presence and the rush of wind were all the warning she received. Someone grabbed her from behind, wrapping an arm around her neck.

There was no doubt as to his intention—to choke her to death.

Her pulse skyrocketed. Heart pounded.

But Chief Winters's words penetrated the fear that gripped her mind and body.

First, don't panic. Take slow, deep breaths to relax. Then assess what is happening. But do it quickly. A quick reaction can save you.

Breathe. She had to breathe. *Hard to do. When. He's. Choking. Me.*

Second, grab his arms. Drop your weight.

She let herself drop, but his grip didn't waver.

Stomp on his foot.

Jewel jabbed her heel into his foot. Then she tried to move. That was the whole point. Move and slam her fist into his groin. But he kept her pinned tightly.

She couldn't budge. Her stomp made no noticeable difference. Again. She tried again.

Next she raised her arm, preparing to turn into her attacker and strike him with her elbow. She'd practiced this and had been successful in class demonstrations. But her attacker seemed to expect her every move and squeezed her tighter, holding her in a vice.

Breathe.

She couldn't breathe.

Darkness edged her vision. Bright pinpoints of light sparked across her eyes.

She struggled and twisted. Had to try something else.

If you can't get away, try to head butt. Grab his ears, nose, anything to gain an escape.

Jewel threw her head forward and then back against her attacker's face. His grip loosened enough for Jewel to break free. She pushed forward and away. Took off running as she gasped for oxygen. No time to stop or even scream.

Had to put distance between them. Escape. She had to get away.

She ran for the only exit.

But he slammed into her back. Toppled her. Jewel fell forward, her body slamming hard against the floor. Pain sliced through her, exacerbating her previous injuries. His body weight pressed heavily against her. His breath was hot across her neck.

God, please, no!

Lungs still burning, Jewel screamed, releasing what little air she'd grabbed.

She couldn't catch her breath, but there were two things she needed to know. "Who are...you? What do you want?"

Voices resounded from below.

Katy and Meral had heard the ruckus.

Jewel tried to scream again to let them know where she was. "Help—"

Boxes toppled, slamming down on her bruised body. Crashing into her head.

Darkness engulfed her.

FOUR

It was late afternoon by the time Colin steered his Jeep up to the B and B. Terry headed back to the police station to finish paperwork, and Cade headed home to his son, little Scotty, and wife, Leah, who was pregnant with their second child. But David had ridden along with Colin and would pick up his truck and Katy, his grandmother. Colin stepped from his Jeep and studied the house. Picturesque and peaceful. A bald eagle soared above the property. Trees rustled in a cooler-than-usual August breeze.

David climbed from the Jeep and walked around, waiting on Colin. "Quiet on the outside. I just hope there's nothing wrong on the inside."

"That makes two of us."

Colin noted David's truck and Jewel's Durango parked to the side. He didn't see Meral and Buck's rental, which caused him concern. Meral had promised to stay with Jewel, but maybe her husband had the car and was running errands in town. Colin had met Meral earlier—as beautiful as her sister but several years younger—but he had yet to meet Buck Cambridge.

He wanted to know more about the husband. Meet the man and get a sense of him. See his interactions with his wife and sister-in-law.

Colin had watched Meral with Jewel and could easily see she loved her sister. In his mind, in his gut, Meral wasn't a suspect, though she'd been conveniently missing, as had her husband, when Jewel had gone into the falls. Regardless, Colin refused to depend on his gut feeling. He'd get the facts.

He and David headed to the porch.

"What are you going to tell her?" David asked.

Jewel would be disappointed they still

knew next to nothing. He didn't like to heap more pain on her injuries.

"I'll reassure her we'll do our best to find whoever did this." Colin opened the front door and stepped into the foyer.

Cell in hand and eyes wide, Meral rushed forward. "Oh, I'm so glad you're here! It's Jewel…" Meral fumbled and dropped her phone, but didn't bend to pick it up. Instead, she ran away.

Colin glanced at David, his heart plunging to his knees, and took off after Meral. "What's happened?" he called after her.

She ran up the stairs and called back to him without pausing. "She's hurt."

And then another flight of stairs.

"But what happened? Does she need medical attention?"

"Maybe. Boxes fell on her. I don't know what happened. We just heard her scream and found her in the attic. I came downstairs to grab my phone and was calling 911 when you came in."

Colin shoved past Meral and climbed the short steps up to the attic, where he found Katy hovered over Jewel. With unshed tears in her eyes, Katy looked at Colin. "She's alive."

Katy moved away and Colin took her place. He shoved the boxes away from Jewel to make more space. None of them were crushingly heavy, but they'd done damage nonetheless. Carefully, he examined her injuries, then realized his mistake.

What am I doing?

He moved out of David's way.

David was a paramedic firefighter, and Colin let him determine if Jewel could be safely moved. David examined her, then started to lift her to carry her from the attic.

"Let me do it." Colin carefully slipped his arms under her neck and knees. Holding Jewel close and tight, Colin stood, kicked junk out of his way and headed for the steps out of the attic.

In the hallway, he glanced at Meral. "Where's her room?"

Meral led him down another set of stairs to the second floor and then into a warm, cozy room decorated with quilts and nautical decor. He gently laid her on a rumpled bed.

"Jewel, wake up." *God, please let her wake up. Please let her be okay.*

"Did you call for help?" he asked. He remembered Meral dropped her cell phone when she'd seen him.

"Well…I was about to. I thought… You're here."

"She needs to see a doctor."

"We could take her in. Would be faster than waiting." David began assessing her injuries, focusing on her head. He had the credentials and experience, after all. Much more than Colin.

Yet Colin didn't want to relinquish Jewel's well-being into anyone else's hands.

"Right here, feels like she has a fresh knot on her head." David moved aside. "She likely has a concussion."

Colin ran his hand over where David indicated, his fingers weaving into her soft hair, searching. "See if you can get Doc Harland out here. I don't think Jewel wants to go back to the hospital."

Katy and David shared a look that he didn't like. He wasn't giving Jewel special treatment. Was he?

"I'll call Doc. See what he wants us to do." David snagged his cell from his pocket and went into the hallway.

While David turned his attention to the call, and Meral and Katy spoke in hushed tones, Colin focused on Jewel. *Lord, please let her be okay.* He didn't think his heart could take any more loss. If he'd thought he'd toughened up enough over the past twenty years since coming to Alaska to flee his bad experience in Texas, he'd been wrong.

Why had this happened on top of yesterday?

"Ladies, please tell me what happened."

Katy pursed her lips. "Well, I don't exactly know. We were in the kitchen."

"I'd come down to get Jewel some tea." Meral frowned.

"I thought we agreed she wasn't to be left alone." He eyed them both.

"But how could I have known that meant I couldn't get her tea? That I couldn't leave her room? Or that *she* couldn't leave her room? I just went to get tea. It shouldn't have been so hard." Meral pressed her face into her hands.

"No need to blame yourself." Guilt hit Colin for being too tough on her. "I'm just trying to protect Jewel and get to the bottom of all this."

"To be fair, dear—" Katy sent a regretful glance Meral's way "—we'd gotten caught up in chatting. Maybe I kept you too long."

"Chief Winters, I'm so sorry this happened," Meral said. "We heard noises coming from above us. I thought I heard someone cry out, so we came first to Jewel's bedroom and that's when we discovered she was gone."

"Then we heard the awful crash." Katy sat on the edge of the bed. "We ran up to the third floor and found the attic door hanging down."

"And so we climbed the steps and found Jewel covered in boxes." Meral fidgeted. Glanced out the bedroom door. Was she waiting on Buck? Wondering where he was? Colin certainly was. This was the second time the man seemed to be missing when Jewel was hurt.

"She could have been crushed." Katy rubbed Jewel's leg as if coaxing her to wake up.

"The boxes weren't heavy enough to crush her." But there she was in the bed, unconscious, regardless. Colin didn't want to think about what could have happened. "I don't know why she'd go to the attic, but she's not in any condition to move around an obstacle course."

A moan escaped Jewel's lips.

He turned his attention back to her. Pressed his hand against her face. Felt her soft skin. "Jewel, can you hear me?"

Her eyelashes fluttered.

"Jewel, wake up. It's me, Colin…er…Chief Winters." His heart was getting the best of him. "Doc Harland is on his way."

He hoped.

"He is," David confirmed from behind.

When her lids finally opened, he could see the pain in her eyes. "I know, hon. I know it hurts."

"Again?" Her question came out in a groan.

"Looks like it, yes. But you're going to be all right. You hear me?"

"No, no, I'm not."

"Don't say that. You're just fine. You have a concussion probably, and a few new bruises, but nothing worse than that. Doc will fix you up right as rain." Colin sounded as if he was grasping for hope.

"Doc can't fix what's wrong with me." Jewel frowned, clearly in pain. "Someone is trying to kill me."

When had Jewel decided she was the specific target?

Colin eased onto the edge of the bed, sitting closer. It should feel wrong, him sitting here like this when Jewel had her sister and Katy Warren to comfort her. What was Colin doing? Hadn't he decided he shouldn't do this? But one close call too many had the protector in him coming out and rearing its big head. The comforter in him that he hadn't realized resided inside was taking over.

"I'll find him. Don't you worry. We went to the waterfall today. We'll find out who did this." He hadn't wanted to bring that up yet since he didn't have any real leads to share, but it was all he could think to do to reassure her. His words portrayed more confidence than he'd felt, though. "In the meantime, you need to rest and recover before you start exploring on your own."

Jewel opened her intense hazel-green eyes and turned them on Colin. His heart jolted in his chest. He couldn't remember a time when his heart jumped into his throat this high, this forcefully. Jewel grabbed his hand on her face. "Don't coddle me, Chief Winters. Forget about the waterfall. He was in my attic."

Surprise mingled with disbelief in the police chief's eyes. That hurt Jewel more than she wanted to admit.

"You've been injured, Jewel." He reclaimed his hand, leaving a cold spot where warmth had been. "You've had a knock on the head. Think about what you're saying."

She wanted to tell him that his words upset her. But then she'd be admitting out loud that his opinion was important. Meral watched her, sympathy carved into her beautiful features. Did she think Jewel had imagined it, too?

"But we were all here. How could someone have been in the house without us knowing about it?" Meral asked.

"How could he have hidden in the attic all this time?" Katy joined the doubters. "We would have heard the noise."

"You *did* hear noise," David said.

"Yes, but only for a minute or so before we heard the crash."

"I thought I heard you scream." Meral pressed her hand over her mouth, eyes wide. "You think…you believe…he was here?"

Jewel grabbed her forehead and slowly sat up, ignoring Chief Winters's protests, along with those of Katy and Meral.

"I don't think. I don't believe. I *know* what I'm saying. I *know* what I saw. I know that I fought an attacker. I know what I experienced before I was knocked out. This time, he tried to strangle me. I got free for a second, only he tackled me before I could reach the door. But I think Meral and Katy scared him off when they responded to my scream and the noise. Maybe he thought he'd killed me. He could have done just that. I should be dead right now."

She turned her eyes to her sister and Katy. "Thank you," she whispered.

Chief Winters lifted her chin, his touch light and gentle. He looked at her neck and his frowned deepened. Then his eyes shot back up to hers, the scolding in them well and alive. "You walked right into that attic without being suspicious or careful. You were told not to go anywhere alone."

She knew he was right, but she couldn't help defending herself. "I'm not accustomed to sitting around and doing nothing. I don't like others waiting on me. I have work to do. Besides, it's the middle of the day and this is my home. I wasn't expecting to find an intruder in the attic."

"You weren't expecting someone to push you into the falls either." He crossed his arms, leveling his gaze.

She turned away, but avoided that stupid mirror. "At least my guests are still out and about. This didn't happen with any of them here."

"And maybe that's the exact reason he thought he could attack you in the middle of the day here in the B and B. That could be the reason he thought he wouldn't get caught.

But at least you got a look at him this time. Do you know who did this?"

"He attacked from behind. The attic was dimly lit, and the small window doesn't give much light. I fought him, but he was strong and finally I had to head butt him to get free. I didn't have time to look back—I just ran, but he toppled me."

She eyed the nightstand drawer, wanting to pull out her Glock and hold it, keep it close, but she didn't want to scare the others. Jewel shook her head and stared at the floor, remembering how it felt to fight for her life. Her breath caught. What good was self-defense if she couldn't win that fight? She fully expected Chief Winters to give her some lecture on the correct moves, what she had and hadn't done right.

Instead, his voice was gentle. "You did well, Jewel, using what you've learned to escape. You can't expect the real experience to be like what we practice in class, though we can try. So take comfort in the fact you're likely alive at this moment because you were able to fight back."

She nodded. It gave her a measure of relief, though not much.

"You called your attacker a he," Chief Winters said. "So you know it's a male this time."

"Yes. Of that I have no doubt."

"Height, weight?"

"Taller than me by half a head or more. Strong, but not muscle-bound. Heavier than me."

Chief Winters resisted the urge to hang his head. Her description wouldn't do them much good, but it was more than they'd had before.

"Just one more question, Jewel."

She rubbed her arms. Doc Harland appeared in the doorway, his brows furrowed.

"What's that?" Jewel directed her question to Chief Winters but stared at that good doctor, wishing he would come in and save her from an interrogation.

"Why did you go to the attic?"

Why indeed.

She must have blanched, because Doc came all the way into the room, looking concerned. "Any more questions can wait until later. If everyone wants to give us some space, and Jewel some privacy, that would be appreciated."

Everyone left except Chief Winters.

Doc gave him a stern nod. "And you, Chief. Can I see my patient alone?"

Chief Winters complied with a frown, but the look he gave Jewel told her she wasn't off the hook. He expected an answer to the question. Jewel didn't have one she felt comfortable delivering.

When he left the room she sighed with relief. Doc Harland paused, stethoscope midair, and looked at her. "It can't be that bad, Jewel. You just relax. This has been too much stress on you. Falling into the river and now taking a tumble in the attic."

How much did Doc Harland actually know? Jewel nodded as he rambled.

"Tell me where you hurt the most."

How could she possibly explain? More than physical pain, the emotional pain of being assaulted in her own home overwhelmed her. There were no words.

And now she could only think of one reason someone had attacked her. Jewel wished she had a confidante. Someone she could trust enough to share her secret. If she'd trusted Silas enough those twenty years ago, then maybe this wouldn't be happening to her now. Maybe someone wouldn't be trying to kill her.

FIVE

Frustration roiled inside as Colin crept up to the attic with a flashlight. He'd have to wait for answers from Jewel, so he'd use the time to see if the attacker had left behind any evidence.

What had Jewel been doing up here? What had been so pressing to drag her out of bed when she'd been through so much already?

Downstairs, Meral had gone to see Katy out. A nurturer, Katy had wanted to stay and help Jewel, but David insisted on taking his grandmother home. Evidently, she was already booked as a babysitter, thanks to Heidi and Isaiah Callahan.

Mountain Cove had some good people, and that encouraged Colin, kept him going when so much else seemed to be deteriorating into chaos and crime. Katy Warren and her entire family were pillars in the community and they had proven themselves to be his friends. He could always count on them.

Katy had that glow about her—loving the great-grandmother years now that they had finally arrived. For too long she hadn't been sure any of her grandchildren would marry. But they were all happily settled now, growing their families with healthy, happy babies for her to spoil. Little wonder she was a spry one for her age.

He only hoped he could be as active when that time came. But if love and family were what kept someone young, then his prospects looked bleak.

He'd never fallen in love and gotten married after losing Katelyn, and he had no legacy. No children. He hadn't allowed himself to think on those things. How did Jewel feel about children? She and her husband had never had them. Had they agreed not to, or was there some other reason? Or had Silas's life been taken from him too soon? That seemed the most probable explanation. As if it was any of Colin's business.

He shoved away the errant thoughts and focused on his investigation and protecting Jewel. He couldn't think of anything that was more important to him at this moment.

In the attic, he flipped on the soft lighting, then added to it as he shined the flashlight beam around where Jewel had fallen. Where the attacker had possibly stood to strangle her. The dusty floor was too disturbed in the scuffle to get any footprints.

Colin wished he had gotten an answer to his question. Why had Jewel come to the attic? Had she heard a noise and come up to investigate? He couldn't believe she would have done that alone after what had happened. Unless she thought it was that raccoon that kept nesting.

That had to be it. She hadn't been thinking about a possible intruder, only about protecting her investment. She needed to start thinking about her safety now. The B and B was secondary. Or was it tertiary now that her sister was back in her life?

Meral held a special place in Jewel's heart, and from a family who had hurt her, too. Disinheriting, disowning someone had to have cut Jewel in a way Colin couldn't fathom. And now the sister and husband had suddenly shown up. Why now, after twenty years? And why was Jewel's life in danger right after they arrived?

He didn't want to rely on instinct, but neither did he believe in coincidence.

Why would the attacker have come to the attic? To hide? Or was there some other reason? Making assumptions was never a good idea. Colin walked around shining the light on boxes and old luggage, trunks, furniture, toys, knickknacks—some of which he'd seen decorating the B and B over the years. She could have come up here to think on moving some things down. One fact he had—

he wouldn't solve this until Jewel answered some very pointed questions. He wished he had a crime-scene division to gather finger-prints. But Mountain Cove had no budget for that. Investigating this would take good, old-fashioned police work. And anyway, gathering prints didn't always give an answer or paint the correct picture.

Colin made his way back downstairs to look around the rest of the house for clues. He was torn between hoping that Doc Harland would give him the free and clear to question Jewel further and hoping he'd be told to leave her alone for a while longer. Every time he looked at her, asked her a question, he felt as though he was beating her up. She needed to recover fully, and Colin wasn't helping.

But she would keep getting hurt until he found the person attacking her. And to track down the culprit, he needed answers.

He heard voices downstairs. A male voice that didn't belong to David. Maybe one of the guests had returned? Or had Meral's husband, Buck, finally shown up?

Colin made his way to the first floor and found Meral in the kitchen in the arms of a man nearing fifty, a good ten if not fifteen years older than Meral, around the same age as Jewel and Colin. They both tensed when they saw him. Meral stepped out of the man's arms.

"Hello, Chief Winters," she said. "This is my husband, Buck Cambridge."

Stepping forward, Colin held out his hand to shake Buck's. The man had a strong grip in return. Well-groomed, graying chestnut-brown hair and a beard framed his mostly square, tanned face. About the same height as Colin—five foot eleven. Stocky but solid. Brown eyes stared back at him, measuring. Gauging.

A strange sensation raked over Colin.

Blocking the wariness creeping in, Colin nodded at the sacks on the floor. "Did some shopping?"

Buck laughed, the sound so jarringly familiar that Colin had to take a steadying step back as he listened. He couldn't put his finger on the associations he had with that laugh, but he knew they weren't good.

"We thought we'd hike the Bledsoe Glacier as soon as Jewel is ready. Maybe we can hire a guide and see one of the ice caves." He hugged Meral closer. "We're here in Alaska to see Jewel for the most part. The scenery is just gravy. Had to get the proper clothing and gear to walk on a glacier. Isn't that right?"

"I suppose. Just a tip, you can always rent the gear you need, too."

Displeasure flickered in Buck's eyes. Colin read that to mean the man didn't like being given tips.

Colin tucked that away for later. Good to note.

Doc Harland entered the kitchen and gave as good of a report on Jewel as he could. He introduced himself to Buck, and Colin studied the man further. He used Doc's distraction to gather his composure. He shouldn't have lost it to begin with.

But something was painfully clear. Somehow Colin knew this man. He couldn't remember from where, but every instinct in him told Colin to be on his guard, that this man couldn't be trusted.

He needed to get Jewel alone to find out what she knew about her sister's husband. And he'd need to tread carefully. Jewel hadn't said so, but he could tell her relationship with Meral was fragile as well as vital. He'd seen a light in Jewel's eyes he hadn't seen in years.

That was her sister's doing.

But Meral's husband was giving off nefarious vibes, and the fact that he'd entered this circle near to Colin's heart—Jewel and her B and B—right before trouble had started set off additional warning sirens in Colin's head.

During his conversation with Doc Harland, Buck held Meral close like a possession, not like someone he cherished. He glanced at Colin, and behind the man's gaze, Colin could swear he saw a smirk.

The man recognized Colin, as well. That had to be it.

Colin's gut tensed. He mentally drew the weapon holstered at his hip.

Doc Harland swung his gaze to Colin. "Now, now, Chief Winters. Jewel is going to be all right."

The man had mistaken Colin's expression for concern over Jewel, which meant he wasn't hiding his emotions. At all. He forced a smile and gave the Doc his due, but stayed fully aware of Buck Cambridge standing to his left.

Colin shook the doctor's hand. "You're a good man, Doc, to come out here to check on Jewel. I know you have other patients and responsibilities."

"I make house calls when it's called for. But Chief Winters—" Doc's expression turned sober "—you find who did this. You take care of our Jewel of the Mountain, and I don't mean the B and B."

"I hear you, Doc." Colin watched the man nod to Meral and Buck and head out of the kitchen. He heard the front door to the B and B open and close.

Attuned to every sound, it was as if they all had been waiting for the doctor to leave. When Colin turned his focus completely on Buck, the man appeared prepared. As if he was expecting to be interrogated. But that wasn't an unusual response.

Now to the more serious question. "Buck, have we met before?"

The man laughed. That familiar, unnerving laugh that Colin couldn't place. "I think I'd remember if we had. I've never been to Alaska before meeting Meral."

The man wasn't lying about Alaska. Colin would trust his instincts on that. But Colin hadn't missed the careful way he'd phrased his answer. No, Colin hadn't met Buck in Alaska. But he hadn't lived in Alaska all his life. Suspicions aside, he needed the facts.

How could he leave Jewel alone in the

house with Buck? Her attacker had proved to be much closer than any of them knew. Colin had a feeling he hadn't gone very far. And this time Colin needed to listen to his instincts.

Jewel rested, both to follow Doc Harland's instructions and because she was well and truly exhausted. She'd heal quicker if she'd give her body the chance to recover. But even though she lay still, she couldn't turn off her mind. Too much had happened, and thoughts constantly bombarded her mind. Who was trying to kill her? Was she safe right now? Would others be hurt because of her? Had the man who wanted to kill her followed her into the attic, or had he already been there either hiding or searching?

One of Katy's framed cross-stitched Bible quotations hung on the wall. Jewel had made the right decision in hanging them. She had hoped to plant seeds in the lives of her guests. Give them peace when they had none. And now she was grateful because she was the one who needed that calming reassurance that could only come from the Lord. She read the words from Psalm 23, letting them wrap around her heart.

The Lord is my shepherd, I lack nothing. He makes me lie down in green pastures, he leads me beside quiet waters, he refreshes my soul.

She knew the scripture already, but seeing it on the wall, created with care and love, reminded her there were good people in the world. Loving people. And that God also loved her. Then, finally, she closed her eyes and felt herself drifting to sleep. But a soft knock came at the door. Jewel inwardly groaned. Her lids were heavy, and she kept her eyes closed as if already asleep. Stirring to answer the door would wake her fully.

She heard the door open.

She heard Meral's whisper and Chief Winters's soft reply.

He'd wanted to ask her about why she'd

gone up to the attic. But he'd have to wait for another time, for which Jewel was grateful. She could feel the weight of her past pressing in on her from two floors above behind the plank in the wall.

There hadn't been a raccoon up there.

She hadn't heard a noise.

But had her attacker been in the attic for the same reason as Jewel? Her heart told her yes. But her head still wasn't sure.

To Jewel's surprise, Meral crept all the way into the room and set something next to the bed. The aroma of soup teased Jewel's nose. Chief Winters was there in the room, too, oddly enough. She heard his soft steps, the rustle of his clothes. Felt his presence. His musky scent mingled with the scent of cowboy soup.

She felt his gaze on her face, and her heart cringed at what he must see, but somehow she knew he looked beyond all the damage to the inside. Part of her longed for him to press his hand against her face as he'd done earlier when he'd coaxed her awake.

She couldn't care about him that way. Could not afford to go there with anyone. She was resolved never to give herself away as she had once done. But that didn't make the pain go away. Her determination didn't make it easier.

Meral and Chief Winters left her alone, and Jewel let herself fall the rest of the way to sleep.

Days later things had quieted down, and her bruises were healing. The stiffness and soreness decreased. Though Doc had told her two weeks on the sutures, that was now only days away. She could almost forget what had happened. Almost pretend she was safe now. Except she wouldn't forget. Not until this was over.

Chief Winters had questioned everyone staying at the B and B, including Meral and Buck, about their whereabouts during the attacks. Jewel had successfully evaded his question about the attic.

Patience had ridden the waves of emotion in his eyes. He very likely could wait her out. But Jewel wasn't sure she would ever be ready to tell him what she wanted to forget. Not unless she was sure her past had anything to do with her attacks. If it didn't, then her secret could remain buried.

There was always a police officer sitting in his vehicle outside, and twice a day he did a walk through the B and B per Chief Winters's orders. A rash of burglaries in Mountain Cove had drawn away the chief's personal attention. She could tell he was frustrated he couldn't be by her side every minute, but why he felt so personally invested in her safety, she refused to examine. It was best she wasn't with him too much.

A plainclothes officer always checked the house after the day's departing guests had left in the morning, and just after they arrived and settled in for the evening for additional security. But never to disturb or cause anyone concern. She found the gesture both frustrating and endearing. It somehow felt like overkill, but also reminded Jewel that her attacker was still out there and could try again.

Tracy and Katy had volunteered to come in to help Jewel's regular employees, Jan and Frances. She thought they secretly wanted to keep an eye on her. So the chores had been done early, and dinner was already simmering in the slow cookers without any effort from Jewel. She should be grateful, but instead, she felt almost smothered. She couldn't stay cooped up like this forever. Like the B and B had been turned into some sort of safe house. It made her wonder if Chief Winters was trying to repair his reputation. Restore the citizens' perception of Mountain Cove as a safe town.

But she made a decision.

This was absolutely the last day she would

stay in her room resting, reading books or watching television.

Meral and Buck had gone out snorkeling with Sylvie and Will Pierson this morning. They had returned earlier than Jewel would have expected from the excursion. Funny to think of calling Billy Pierson *Will* now, but that was what Sylvie, his new bride, called him, and the rest of the town had caught on. She'd moved here after they'd got engaged and they'd married quickly. Even before the wedding, Will and Sylvie had added a scuba diving tour business to his bush piloting. It made Jewel happy to think two opposites like that could be together. Reminded her that obstacles could be overcome when two people knew how to love each other. She'd had that once.

And a freak lightning strike had taken it from her.

She thought back to Chief Winters's words to her in the hospital right after the fall.

"Accidents happen, Jewel. People fall where

they shouldn't all the time, including in the shower, where some die every year."

He'd been attempting to reassure Jewel. Convince her she had no blame in what he'd thought then had been merely an accident. Jewel had said similar words to Tracy when she'd needed reassurance that her attacker would be caught and she would be safe. Those words, that conversation, came back to haunt Jewel now.

"We'll get him before he takes someone else down."

"You can't promise that, Jewel."

"No, I can't. But there are no promises in life. People die every day, people who don't have a killer after them. I lost my husband a few years back. He was a firefighter— he mentored David Warren, in fact. But he didn't die fighting a fire. No. He had to get struck by lightning while he was hiking in the mountains. A lightning strike killed my husband."

There were no guarantees in life, but Jewel

knew she could count on lightning striking again in the form of her attacker. The question was—would he succeed in killing her the next time?

A car door slammed outside, and she glanced out the window to see Buck driving away.

There was no time to lose. Jewel went down into the kitchen. She had things to do. Questions to ask.

As soon as they spotted her, Tracy, Katy and Meral suddenly stopped talking, and each tried to hide a guilt-ridden expression, as though they'd been talking about Jewel.

Tracy stepped forward, concern in her gaze. "Jewel, how are you doing?"

Jewel waved away her concerns. "I'm sick of sitting around. Resting is overrated."

She smiled, trying to persuade them she was much improved. Given that her purple bruises had turned to a sickly green, she wasn't surprised that her appearance didn't convince them.

"Where's Buck?" she asked as casually as she could, grabbing an apple, but out of nowhere it sounded strange. She'd seen him leave and wanted to make sure he wouldn't be back for some time.

Meral's eyes widened. "I don't know. He went exploring, looking for a creek to fish in, I think."

If Buck wasn't here, then now was a good time to ask the questions burning inside. "Meral, I can't tell you how happy it's made me that you've come here to see me, to find me. I hate all the years that have been wasted."

Meral slid into the chair at the kitchen table. "We don't have to think about that. We have each other now."

With so much riding on the answers to her questions, Jewel could only offer a tenuous smile. "Meral...I...I need to know."

Her sister reached over and grabbed Jewel's hand. "What do you need, Jewel? Anything. I'll tell you anything."

Jewel's throat grew tight, her mouth suddenly dry. Her sister loved her, and the suspicions running through Jewel filled her with shame.

"Why, after all these years, did you decide to find me? To come and see me? Why now?"

Her sister's mouth dropped open. Then, "I don't understand what you're asking."

Jewel could see that she had approached her need to find answers in the wrong way. She was messing this up. Her fear was seeping through, affecting how she came across. She sat in a chair across from Meral, trying to dial down the tension.

"What's this all about?" Katy squeezed Meral's shoulder and gave Jewel a gentle but questioning look.

Honestly, Jewel wished she could have some privacy with her sister, but she never found herself alone with Meral after the attacks. And if the other women were gone, Buck was around and wouldn't let Meral out of his sight. Jewel had no choice but to forge ahead.

"Did you ever think about coming to see me over the years? Ever think about finding me? A phone call? An email or a letter?" Jewel regretted the accusing tone.

Meral pursed her lips, wounded surprise in her gaze. "I could ask you the same."

"Of course I did. But I was hurt, so hurt. I don't think I even realized it until you showed up at my door, and you weren't even to blame. I got caught up in living life in Alaska and loving my husband and—" Jewel hung her head, regret clinging to her heart "—and trying to forget I even had a family."

Jewel lifted her gaze to meet her sister's beautiful eyes. "I'm so sorry now, for everything."

"I thought we decided to put the past away, Jewel, and move forward. You need to quit beating yourself up. I forgive you, and I hope you forgive me for not trying harder to stay in touch. But when I was young, I idolized you. Looked up to you. Then you decided to leave us all behind for Silas. I thought you didn't love me or care about me. It's taken me years to get over that, but like you, I got busy with college and then fell in love and got married the first time. I tried not to think about the sister I'd loved and lost. The sister who had hurt me."

"Was it your idea, Meral?" Jewel finally asked. "Was it your idea to come and see me now?"

Meral put her elbows on the table and pressed her face into her hands. "I don't understand why it matters whose idea it was. Buck knew that I missed you. He knew our family's history. He found you for me. But I wanted to come. Like you, I didn't realize how much I'd missed you or I couldn't admit it, until Buck surprised me with this trip as a wedding present. I can't think of a better gift. Or a better husband. I hope you're not hurt that I didn't initiate the trip. I hope all that matters is that we've found each other. Let's never let anything come between us again." Meral reached for Jewel's hand.

Or anyone, Jewel wanted to say, but she knew that was impossible.

"I'm not hurt." Jewel hung her head, knowing she'd caused her sister pain. Fearing she might lose her when she'd only just found her if she pressed further. She couldn't bring herself to risk their tentative truce by asking Meral if she'd known what Jewel had taken all those years ago, and if she'd told Buck. Not now, and definitely not with Tracy and Katy looking on.

"I'm going to take a long hot bath." Jewel stood, feeling as though the stiffness and aches had returned with a vengeance. "Just letting you know in case you knock on my door and I don't answer."

Jewel left her friends and her sister and climbed the stairs to her room. Coming here had been Buck's idea. Not the answer she'd wanted to hear. But an answer that could bring her closer to the truth about who had attacked her.

SIX

She ran the bath water, poured in bubble bath and let it rise. Shut off the water and left the bathroom, shutting the door behind her. She would take that bath.

Later.

Now she crept up another flight of stairs and then climbed the ladder into the attic. This time she'd brought a flashlight to chase away the shadows that remained after she turned on the light. At least the dormer window offered a little more illumination. She glanced at every dark corner of the place, positioned a board over the entrance so she'd hear anyone who might try to come inside, though she was certain her attacker couldn't be in the house this time.

Jewel crept all the way back, stepping around boxes and trunks and memories. Once she was on the other side of this trouble—if she came out of it alive, that was—she needed to spend time organizing the attic. Switch out decor downstairs again. Carefully, Jewel stepped so she didn't make too much noise and worry Tracy, Katy and Meral all over again.

She swiped away the dust along the wall looking for that plank. Could it have been so long ago that she couldn't remember exactly where she'd hidden it away? It should be here, yet the plank wouldn't budge.

Propping the flashlight just right, Jewel used both fingers, sliding her fingernails between the boards. She dug her fingertips into the crack as leverage and tried to work the plank loose until she finally felt the slightest shift in the board.

Pain stung her finger. Jewel snatched her hand back. A sliver had caught under the skin. She spotted a nail on the floor and picked it up. Poking it into the crack, she twisted and angled it, working it back and forth until the board shifted enough so she could grab it.

There.

She tugged and twisted the plank that fought back. It didn't seem to want to give up its resting place after twenty-some years. That, she understood. She had been comfortable, too, letting her secret stay hidden. That was until Meral and Buck had shown up. Now she had to look back in order to move forward.

Finally, she removed the cranky old board entirely.

And there inside the hole in the wall rested the box.

Emotion punched her stomach so hard she gasped. She hadn't considered the effect this would have on her. Tears spilled down her cheeks. Long pent-up anguish, regret and pain poured out of her. She had never allowed herself to give up the grief, to cry over her mistake, to truly put it behind her. Until now, she had never regretted her decision. She hadn't allowed herself the luxury.

Now, twenty years later, she realized her mistake. She'd been young and impressionable and reckless when she'd left her wealthy family behind for love. Left her dreams and career pursuits behind.

But she'd met Silas Caraway, and it seemed as though all the plans she'd made were nothing compared to loving him. She'd known that Silas wasn't the kind of man her family expected her to marry. Her parents had had big plans for her in terms of carrying on the Simmons family name and legacy in Simmons Diamonds.

Jewel had been warned that once she left, she wouldn't be allowed to come back. She wouldn't see a dime from the estate and wouldn't be assisted if needed. Shocked by the pronouncement, she'd been terrified of the risks her future held, yet she hadn't been able to turn her back on love. So Jewel had stolen a valuable family heirloom when she'd left, keeping it tucked away in hiding as a safety net.

Just in case.

What if things hadn't worked out with Silas in Alaska?

She'd been willing to give up her lavish lifestyle for love. Believed what she had with her husband was strong. But it never hurt to have a backup plan. Except she'd never told her husband that she'd kept anything belonging to her family. After what they'd put her through, it would have seemed to him as though she hadn't trusted him enough. He would have seen her need to have a backup plan as proof that she'd expected their marriage to fail.

How that would have hurt him. She hadn't wanted him to ever know. Therefore she couldn't keep the diamond in a safe-deposit box in the bank of a small town, because he would have found out eventually. She'd found an adequate hiding place in the big old house.

She tugged out the box, her heart pulsing erratically.

After wrapping her fingers around it, she opened the box and stared at the Krizan Diamond, a glistening yellow stone cut from one of the Golconda diamonds—an ancient mine in India. The diamond had been handed down through the generations in Jewel's mother's family.

How it still shimmered a vivid yellow, the color increasing the value of the 20.25-carat stone.

Though only one of many such family diamonds, how silly of her to take it. Had someone reported it stolen? Was insurance filed on it? Doubtful she could have ever sold it without everyone knowing the truth of her crime unless she dipped her fingers into the black market somehow and found a collector. Odd the things people did when they were young.

Today, she never would have done such a thing. But she was older and wiser.

This had to be why someone wanted to kill

her. It was valuable enough to be a powerful temptation to someone greedy and ruthless. But who knew she'd taken it? Who knew she had it? She suspected her mother had known she took the diamond, but Jewel couldn't see her mother telling anyone, not when it might get Jewel into trouble. Jewel had always imagined that when she'd seen her mother peeking out the window as Jewel had left with Silas, she'd seen the glimmer of approval in her eyes; had chosen to believe that her mother would have wanted her to have this security.

But maybe she had fooled herself. How could she have been so naive to hope that no one else in the family would realize she'd taken it?

Did her sister know?

Doubts filled her about the man Meral loved and had married. Had Meral told Buck about the diamond?

Her hands trembled.

But then it hit her afresh. She still possessed the Krizan Diamond—a stone worth millions—and all it represented to her were fear and guilt. The diamond's value, the danger she likely had brought on herself by possessing it, struck her like a bolt from the sky and singed her skin. She dropped it, letting it fall into the box.

She placed the rudimentary container back into its hiding place.

Jewel pushed the plank into place and quietly shoved boxes in front of the wall. If someone were searching in here, it would be easy enough to discover where she had disturbed the dust. She'd need to clean the entire attic to cover her tracks. But what was she thinking?

It was too late. Her attacker had already found her in the attic—already knew that that was where to look to uncover her secrets.

A noise disturbed her thoughts—the board over the entrance to the attic. Panic sent Jewel's pulse racing. She grabbed the flashlight and ran to the entrance. Best to take the offensive move while she had the high ground.

"Don't move," she said.

"Or what?" Chief Winters stared up at her. "You're going to hit me with a flashlight?"

"Chief Winters."

She dropped the flashlight, her only weapon. She should have brought the Glock. Clearly, she wasn't ready for any serious self-defense. He was probably disappointed in his student. She started down, but Chief Winters stepped up and Jewel inched back as he climbed the ladder until he was standing in the attic with her.

"What a surprise that I should find you in the attic again."

She hadn't wanted to answer questions about the first time she'd come, and she'd managed to evade him—but there would be no escaping him now. Of course, he would have to stand much too close.

Jewel's pulse hadn't slowed since she'd

heard the noise. What was he doing standing so near? His proximity made her tremble.

She sucked in a calming breath. She should take a step back, but she couldn't move. Instead, she hung her head, feeling like a teenager when she was anything but. Something about this man sent her heart racing and tumbling around inside. He lifted her chin with his finger.

What was he doing?

She wanted to tell him what a romantic cliché his action was, but then she'd be admitting that the moment felt like something out of a romance novel, because she was attracted to him. And she couldn't admit that to him or to herself. She would never risk her heart again. Even if she were willing, her family heirloom stood between them.

She was a thief.

He was the law.

A beam of sunlight streaked through the dirty window, illuminating the dust motes dancing around them.

"What are you doing up here again? And by yourself?" His sharp blue eyes turned dark.

What should she tell him? She couldn't share what she'd done with anyone, especially him. Not yet. "Chief Winters." His name came out in a desperate tone.

His gaze softened. "Jewel, don't you think it's about time you call me Colin? I can see you calling me by my title when we're around others, out of respect, but we're alone now. We've been friends long enough, haven't we?" He finally dropped his hand. "There's no need to be so official with me all the time."

Her heart rate jumped higher. Jewel had thought he would press her for answers. His suggestion was the last thing she'd expected.

His voice was so gentle, so endearing, Jewel could almost forget he was here on official business. That was *why* he was here, wasn't it? A knot twisted in her throat. Calling him by his official title, thinking about him only as the police chief, helped her to protect herself, to keep her resolve to never fall again. If she could fall for anyone, it would be this man.

But would it be so bad to call him by his name? "Colin...I..."

"There." He grinned. "Was that so hard?"

Her heart tilted. She opened her mouth to speak—

A woman's scream broke through the attic.

Jed Turner, the officer Colin had stationed at the B and B today, was facedown in the woods near the house. Colin knelt by Jed and checked for a pulse, though he already knew what he would find. The man was dead.

Still kneeling by the fallen officer, Colin's gut churned as he searched the woods that grew thicker in the distance. The murderer was long gone.

Colin's heart was a chunk of lead in his chest. Jed was in his late fifties, only a few years away from retiring. He had a wife, Clara, plus two grown kids and three grandchildren. Though Jed's troubles were over,

Colin would now have to face his wife and give her the news, a task he didn't relish. The absolute worst part of his job.

What had happened to draw his officer into the woods after Colin had instructed him, after Colin's own arrival, to leave?

Colin thought about Buck Cambridge. From the moment they'd met, something about Buck had made Colin think of a venomous, wild creature that would bite if pressured.

Had that feral creature—a human in this instance—been pressured to bite? Killing a police officer would only up the stakes and bring on a full-out manhunt. Obviously, Jed must have seen something incriminating, discovered something to identify Jewel's attacker.

Colin glanced behind him at the others who had gathered, waiting at the edge of the woods. Jewel hugged herself, her face twisted in anguish. Next to her Katy and Tracy, Meral and Buck, hovered and comforted each other over this new development.

Colin stood, wanting to search the woods, but he wouldn't leave them alone. He hiked back to his vehicle and called for backup and for the retrieval of Jed's body.

Jewel approached him. "I'm so sorry, Colin."

He couldn't begin to convey in words the anger, grief and guilt roiling inside. Add to that hearing his name on her lips again, and he realized he must have been nuts to ask her to say it. It made him all kinds of crazy, and he knew better.

He *knew* better.

Katelyn's death, her murder, had happened because Colin had been emotionally involved. That should be enough warning for him. He pulled his gaze from Jewel's torn features. If he looked at her any longer, he'd pull her right into his arms. Not to comfort her but to comfort himself, something he didn't deserve in the face of Jed's death.

"For what, Jewel? This wasn't your fault."

"Yes, it is. Someone is trying to kill me. To

get to me. And now Jed Turner is dead because he was protecting me."

His radio squawked and Colin answered, detailing the events to Terry Stratford, who was headed this way. There'd been a skirmish in town, but Terry had settled it. Skirmishes were preferred over murder.

Colin glanced at Buck Cambridge, who held a crying Meral against him. The man had checked out when Colin had looked into his background. Was clean. No priors. He was a simple businessman. An import-export consultant. Those were the facts, and Colin could only use those, but his gut told him there was more to the man. Something dangerous, sinister.

He allowed his gaze to fall on Jewel again as she comforted Katy and Tracy. He needed to convince Jewel to leave Mountain Cove for a while, until he could get this taken care of. She wasn't safe here. Her friends and family—namely Meral—had promised to stay close. Everyone wanted to protect her, yet he'd found her alone in the attic. Alone. *Again.*

And now no one was in the house. Colin would have to check every nook and cranny before he let anyone back inside.

What if Colin hadn't been here? Hadn't been up in the attic with Jewel?

He slipped his hand around her arm, drew her away from the others and kept his voice low. "You need to leave, Jewel. You can't stay here anymore." Colin wasn't sure he trusted himself to protect her anymore either. He was failing at his job, after all.

Again...

He didn't want to think about the past, but the images drifted through him like shadows all the same.

"This is my business. My livelihood. I can't leave. There are guests to take care of. And Meral's here. You don't have any idea how much that means to me. I can't just leave."

With Jed's death it was clear there could be collateral damage—that others around Jewel were in harm's way. Didn't she see that? But where could she go that was safe? He'd tried to create a safe house at her B and B.

Her striking hazel-green eyes were usually so transparent, filled with warmth and care and honesty, but that was all shuttered away from him now. He didn't like it. Jewel was purposely hiding something from him. Disappointment in her, in the situation, nearly overshadowed Jed's death.

But in her gaze he saw something else. What he never expected to see. Never wanted to see. Jewel was disillusioned with his abilities. She wanted him to do his job and catch this guy, felt let down that he hadn't done so already. He saw in her eyes the lack of trust and faith that he'd seen in the mayor's eyes, in the city-council members.

Colin released her arm. Pulled the knife from his heart that Jewel hadn't even known she'd stabbed into him and twisted.

He was getting too emotionally involved, more so than would do either of them any good. How did he protect her? Colin wished now that she would call him Chief Winters again, for both their sakes. He needed to ask the hard question, and his emotions stood in the way of that, too, but Jewel would die, others would die—as someone already had—if he didn't ask.

"When I came to you in the hospital, I asked you if you knew who had pushed you into the waterfall. At the time, I thought maybe you were a random victim. Simply at the wrong place at the wrong time. But now I think we both know that's not the case, and I'm going to ask you again, do you have any idea who would want to kill you? And if not who, then *why* someone would want to kill you?"

Jewel hesitated as though considering his questions.

Cruisers pulled into the B and B drive along with the ambulance that would take Jed's body. Given the murder of a police officer, Colin would be calling in the Alaska State Troopers on this investigation. Meral and Buck approached Jewel, apparently wanting to protect family. Either that or interfere with his investigation. Colin was running out of time to get answers.

"Someone died today, Jewel. If you know something that you're not telling me, I need you to tell me now so I can stop this before someone else dies. Before they come for you again. I'll put two officers on the house and on you this time, but we'll be better prepared, better able to face an attack if we know what we're looking for. I need more information if I'm going to catch this guy."

Finding the murderer would be the best way to end this.

"Is everything okay?" Meral put her hand on Jewel's shoulder and squeezed. Buck hovered just behind.

Jewel nodded, pressing a hand over her sister's. To Colin she said, "I don't know who's after me."

He frowned. He'd thought Jewel was about to tell him something before her sister ap-

proached. Did she understand she was putting others' lives at risk and prolonging the
risk to herself? He gave her a hard look.

"If you think of anything, you know where
to reach me."

SEVEN

Jewel watched out the front window, grateful the ambulance and the last police cruiser had finally left. Well, that wasn't entirely true. An unmarked police car was parked outside, two officers dressed in plain clothes now walked the grounds and stayed in the extra rooms in the B and B—the rooms vacated by guests due to the murder.

Other officers still searched the woods near the house, looking for clues to find a killer.

All the police activity was sure to ruin her business, but she cared about Jed's family more than her business. He'd lost his life because of her. Would one of her guests be next? Should she set it all out for them this evening as each of them returned from their outings so they knew the risks?

She pushed down the anxiety swirling inside. How had it come to this?

It would be so much easier if she knew who was trying to kill her instead of just having suspicions that she hoped and prayed weren't true. Suspicions she was holding at bay against all reason. If she knew for certain, then she wouldn't be so torn about telling Colin everything. It felt strange to think of him as Colin now instead of Chief Winters. But it also felt natural, and that particular wall she'd erected as a safety net was already broken down. In fact, when he'd assigned his officers to stay and watch the house, Jewel had been disappointed—she had wanted Colin to stay.

Being near him was dangerous. She should be relieved he'd left, but the relief didn't resolve her disappointment that he'd chosen to assign guard duty to his officers.

Jewel sighed. She was losing her mind.

After Colin had checked the house to ensure her safety, he'd nodded at her just before he'd walked out the door. His demeanor had told her that he was also disappointed in her. Maybe even angry with her. She'd never seen that look in his eyes—he knew she was holding back, purposely hiding information.

A man had been killed because of Jewel, and she wanted to keep her secret?

Despite Colin's frustration with her, he hadn't pressured her to give more than she'd been willing.

Her heart shifted, inched toward him. How could it not?

She wanted to shove aside her fears, confess what she'd done in the past and tell him her suspicions. Tell him what someone could be after. But Meral and Buck had been right there when he'd asked, and then Meral had promised to stay with her at all times.

Behind Jewel, her sister sat on the sofa and chatted on the phone. Jewel had no idea where Buck had sauntered off to now. She hoped he wasn't in the attic searching for the diamond.

She dropped the curtain and plopped on the sofa. Though absorbed in her phone call to a friend in Baltimore, Meral glanced at Jewel, her brows drawing together. Jewel didn't want to concern Meral with her anguish, so once again she turned her attention to the window.

Guilt chewed at her insides, making her forget about her stitches and bruises. For years she'd been dishing out advice and words of wisdom to friends and even to guests when they confided in her. Jewel had always thought that was her one gift, but now when it came to her own life, wisdom escaped her. Everything was twisted into a ball that she had no idea how to untangle. What right did she have to give advice when she harbored such a secret?

Maybe she was trying too hard to figure it out on her own so she could protect herself. There was only one thread for her to pull.

One thing to do, and then let things unravel as they would.

I have to talk to him. Tell him everything.

Jewel made her decision. She stood from the sofa and tried to get Meral's attention, but Meral lifted a finger for Jewel to wait. Instead, Jewel went to her room and changed. She rummaged through her dresser for makeup, which she hardly ever wore except on special occasions like Christmas. This wasn't a special occasion, but her reflection was gaunt and, frankly, terrified her. What was it doing to others? Making them think she was weaker than she was? Vulnerable? Well, Jewel was strong, and she was ready to make a stand.

Ready to end this once and for all.

A knock came at her door. "It's Meral."

"Come in."

Her sister stepped inside. "What are you doing? Where are you going?"

"I need to go to town and talk to Colin... Chief Winters."

Her sister's frown turned into a soft smile. "You like him, don't you?"

Meral's words surprised Jewel. Her sister hadn't been here long enough to know that, had she? "What makes you say that?"

"I have eyes. Besides, he likes you, too, Jewel."

Jewel didn't say anything to Meral's comment. Just worked to cover her haggard appearance with concealer. Spiffed up her bobbed hair that was more difficult to deal with than when it had been long. Funny, she'd cut it to make life simpler. Maybe Meral thought she was trying to look good for the chief of police. Jewel paused. Was she?

Well, Jewel was about to put an end to that once and for all. Once he knew the truth, Colin—Chief Winters—couldn't like her anymore. She would drive a much-needed wedge between them with her words. But she feared she would also drive a wedge between her and Meral, losing two people she cared about deeply in one fell swoop.

"You can't go alone, you know. I'm happy to ride along."

Jewel sighed. She'd never felt more smothered. "I need some air." Some space.

She was going through the motions, hoping she'd get up the nerve to actually go through with telling Colin about her past and her suspicions. She could be way off base and sharing a secret she didn't want anyone to know. Implicating a man who might be innocent. Meral would be devastated and would leave, then Jewel would never see her again.

Jewel put her brush in the drawer and eyed her sister in the mirror. For all Jewel knew, Meral was also after the diamond. Had their parents threatened to disinherit her for marrying Buck, cutting her off completely, just as they had Jewel for marrying Silas? Jewel frowned and averted her gaze.

"What's wrong, Jewel?" Meral asked.

She shook away her misgivings. "Nothing."

"Let me tell Buck where we're going and that I'm riding with you."

No! No, don't...

But she couldn't stop Meral. Couldn't tell her the reasons for her uncertainty.

Nor should Jewel be afraid of her own sister, yet her hands trembled. She stood tall and tried to project confidence into her words. "We'll just okay it with the officers first, but I'm sure it will be fine. I'm heading into town to the police station to talk to Chief Winters. How could they object to that?"

Maybe on the way Jewel could somehow bring up the topic and ask Meral what she knew about the diamond. Yes. This was a good thing, after all. Jewel would finally be alone with Meral without anyone around to hear them.

"Let me freshen up and grab my purse," Meral said. "I'll let Buck know. He's taking a nap. All this excitement has been draining to both of us, as I'm sure it has been to you."

That was an understatement.

"I'll meet you downstairs," Jewel waited until Meral was gone, then slipped the Glock out of the drawer in her nightstand and into her bag.

Her efforts at self-defense hadn't worked that well. She couldn't count on those skills. Still, she hoped she wouldn't be forced to use the gun. Silas had taught her about using weapons, and she was a decent marksman. Living on the edge of the wilderness, she needed to know how to use a gun in case a wild animal accosted her or a guest. But Jewel hadn't wanted to use such a deadly weapon to protect herself from another human being, hence the self-defense classes.

At any rate, now she would be doubly armed, if she counted her meager self-defense skills. Wouldn't it be nice to face off with her attacker, Jed's killer, and end this once and for all?

She could almost pray she would see the man again today. Almost.

As it turned out, arming herself didn't matter. Officer Roberts wouldn't let her drive into town without him. She would go crazy if this didn't end soon. Because he was driving Jewel, Meral decided to stay behind after Buck asked her to. Not that Jewel could have had her conversation in the same vehicle with Officer Roberts.

Jewel got into her old Dodge Durango, and Officer Roberts rode in the passenger seat, leaving the unmarked vehicle behind for the officer remaining at the house. As she steered along the bumpy drive on her property to the road back to town, Jewel's palms grew moist. She felt uncomfortable, as though Officer Roberts was watching her every move, scrutinizing her for some mistake. But it had been days since she'd gotten the concussion. She was fine now.

Except that she was nervous under Officer Roberts's gaze as though she were guilty of some crime.

Well...

Maybe the officer was still unhappy that she had insisted on going. When she had first told him that she wanted to drive to the station, he had demanded that she tell him what she wanted to say to Chief Winters, and then he would relay the information.

Jewel had had to stand her ground and remind him that she wasn't a prisoner in her home, and she was going to town with or without him. He was a younger officer. Nice and friendly. But she had given him a choice. He could go along or not, but she would only speak to Colin. Chief Colin Winters was the only person she could trust with her secret, though she knew he would be more than conflicted with the news. If it helped them solve the murder of an officer, to catch the killer before he struck again, then Jewel had to reveal her past.

I can do this.

Have to be strong. Stronger than I've ever been.

It surprised her just how hard this was going to be.

"You seem very tense, Mrs. Caraway, if you don't mind me saying so."

"It's Jewel, please. Everyone calls me Jewel."

"Yeah, even the chief, I noticed."

"We've known each other a long time." Jewel noted that Officer Roberts didn't ask her to call him by his first name, which was Matt. She stifled a chuckle. He'd want to keep himself official, especially when he was working, which she understood.

"Well, Jewel, you seem nervous to me. Are you sure you don't want me to drive? You can pull over, and I'll drive and you can relax."

"You promised you wouldn't give me a ticket if I messed up." She forced a laugh. "I just need to drive, to feel like I'm free. To do something with my hands."

"I understand." Officer Roberts stiffened next to her. His hand fisted around the handgrip on the door.

She picked up speed as she drove a lonely stretch of road with a great view of the mountains and the glistening blue waters of the channel, as well as the town of Mountain Cove, in the distance. This scenic drive into town was one of the reasons Silas had bought the property. Jewel let herself smile, if only for a moment.

"How's your family doing?" she asked, wanting to keep Office Roberts talking. She knew his parents had moved to Mountain Cove from Juneau when he was in his early teens and now he was a police officer. They had to be proud. Maybe a normal conversation would relax him *and* her.

"Watch out!" Officer Roberts yelled, then grabbed the steering wheel.

At the same moment, Jewel saw the grill of a big-wheeled black Suburban heading straight for them from the woods across the road. She punched the gas pedal to move them out of the way at the same time Officer Roberts yanked the wheel to the right.

The Suburban slammed into them.

Behind her, metal crunched and twisted.

She could have been killed instantly had Officer Roberts not reacted. But it wasn't over yet. The Suburban kept pushing, tires grinding and squealing as the Durango slid dangerously toward the edge of the drop-off.

She couldn't get out, and before Officer Roberts could open his own door, the Durango rolled onto the passenger side. Jewel's body jerked to the right, and she hung there, her seat belt keeping her in place. The vehicle tilted, hesitated.

Jewel screamed.

Officer Roberts yelled, "Hold on!"

The momentum rolled them over again. Now they hung upside down as the Durango tilted and rolled again.

And again.

In slow, wavering revolutions.

Each roll had Jewel squeezing her eyes, gasping for breath as she prayed for their lives.

The cab of the Durango shrank, the ceiling punching in as the weight of the vehicle slammed against hard ground and rock with each turn.

Finally, the Durango stopped with a jolt

after crushing against a tree on the passenger side and jarring every bone in her body with the impact. She could only be grateful they had stopped rolling.

Am I still alive?

Her heart beat wildly against her rib cage. Definitely, she was alive, but for how much longer? She felt the ache across her chest from the seat belt for what would surely become another bruise.

She released a half sigh, half cry, then looked at Officer Roberts. "Are you okay? We have to get out of here."

But he didn't respond.

Oh, no. God, please, no. They'd hit a tree, which could have been deadly. She thought of the boy he had been. The parents who had raised him.

Bracing herself, Jewel released her seat belt and grabbed his arm. He didn't appear to be injured, but it could have been internal. He could simply be unconscious and would wake up with nothing more than a concussion. Jewel wished, hoped and prayed it so.

Pebbles and dirt trickled down from above. The telltale sounds of someone coming, scrambling down, echoed.

Oh, no!

She shook the police officer. "He's coming," she whispered. "We have to get out of here."

But it was no use. Officer Roberts didn't wake up.

She searched for her purse, where she'd stuck the Glock, but it was out of sight and reach, crushed somewhere in the twisted vehicle. Officer Roberts was dressed in regular clothes. She hadn't seen where he kept his weapon. Didn't see it now, or any communication device. She'd search him if she had to, but she'd prefer if he woke up.

She and Officer Roberts both had been fortunate to survive the initial impact and subsequent rolls, but how could they stay that way? If they couldn't get out of this vehicle and away from the man who'd run them off the road, they both would die.

Then he stirred.

"We have to get out of here," she whispered. "He's coming."

Officer Roberts groaned. "Who? Who's coming?"

The man who pushed me into the falls. The man who attacked me in the attic. The man who killed Jed.

"The man driving the Suburban just now. Don't you remember? He pushed us over the edge. He's coming to finish the job! Please, Officer Roberts… Matt…we have to get out."

Finally, he opened his eyes, though he squinted in pain and looked at her. Fear ripped across his features, then he stiffened, coming to himself, projecting himself as an officer of the law. He moved in the seat or tried to. Then his head fell back and he shut his eyes.

"What's wrong? Where are you hurt?"

He glanced down and tried to pull his legs up. "My leg is…I think it's broken…" His words trailed off as pain contorted his voice.

Then he opened his eyes again and peered at her. "Go."

"No. I won't leave you."

He pushed her. "You have to get out of here. I'm not going anywhere. But I can call for help. I have a weapon, so I can protect myself, but I can't protect you. You're in the line of fire, and you need to hide."

"Give me your gun and I'll be the one to protect us both."

He shook his head, his face scrunching with the effort. "No. This could be your only chance to get away. You have to climb out and hide in the woods until help comes. Do as I say before it's too late."

Jewel pressed her foot against the console for leverage and scrambled over the wheel. She tried to shove open the door, but it wouldn't budge. "How do I get out of here? I can't open the door."

"Climb out the dash window." He barely lifted his leg—the good one—and kicked the cracked window out. "Here, you take the Taser. This is a new toy for the department, and I don't much like it anyway."

Jewel wrapped her hands around it. Uncertainty about leaving him behind slowed her exit.

He nodded. "I'll be okay. I'll call for help while you hide. Do not let yourself be caught, and only use the Taser as a last resort. Now go."

Tears pooled in Jewel's eyes. She hesitated.

"We'll both die for nothing if you don't get out of here," he said.

What did he mean? He wasn't expecting to die, was he? Looking at his face, she realized that that was exactly what he expected. And then Jewel knew she had to draw whoever was coming away from Officer Roberts. She didn't want to leave him, but, if anything, she could save him by drawing the attacker away from him.

Jewel climbed out, careful to avoid glass from the windshield. Clinging to the twisted hood of the now-destroyed Durango that she'd had for years, she listened. Nothing. She heard nothing. But she sensed someone watching. Goose bumps rose on her skin.

Was she in his rifle's sights? Is that how he would kill her now?

Her only chance was to climb down from where the vehicle rested against the tree, practically hanging there as the ground dropped away. She studied the terrain. The road above her twisted and curved around a towering mountain that swept into a thick, old-growth forest with eight-hundred-year-old trees. Just beyond, only a few yards from her vehicle, was a granite cliff that dropped into a misty fjord.

If not for the tree, Jewel and Officer Roberts would have gone over. Is that what the killer had intended? Jewel had to hurry. But she worried if she jumped from the Durango she'd slide the rest of the way over the cliff.

Sensing that she had run out of time, Jewel sent up a quick prayer and leaped for her life.

EIGHT

Heart pounding, Jewel hit the ground. Her feet dug into the mossy earth, but they slid out from under her as her momentum pushed her toward the cliff's edge. Dropping the Taser, she grabbed the thick ferns, fingers stripping away fronds. Still she slid. She sank her fingers into the ground, nails gouging the earthy loam.

"Come on!"

She rolled to her back to see her doom. Pebbles and rock and sticks dug into her back as she watched the approaching cliff. She was slowing down, but not enough to save her.

A huge cedar grew off to the side of her path. It could stop her momentum. Just like the tree that had stopped the Durango. Just like the fallen trunk that had grabbed her from the river.

That was her only hope. Jewel stretched and reached, could feel her stitches tearing apart, ripping skin. A scream tore from her mouth as pain sliced through her, but her arms caught the tree and she dug in, held tight as the bark grated across her arms.

Jewel scrambled her legs up the side of the trunk and under her, craving the protection of the tree that had kept her from falling to her death. If only she could stay there.

Pressing her face into bark, drawing in the scent of cedar, she almost wept. But she knew she had no time to catch her breath or gather her composure. Jewel crouched and watched the area near the Durango, searching for the man after her, but she saw no one. She scrambled forward on her knees until the ground leveled out enough that she could stand and took off running to the south toward town. Away from the cliff and the Durango. She could only hope that her absence from the

Durango would draw the attacker after her and away from Officer Roberts, but at the same time she didn't want to be found.

With her injuries, fighting the dense undergrowth was no easy task, but the thick copse of spruce, cedar and hemlock would help her hide.

This was the beauty that had drawn her to Alaska. This was the beauty that would keep her here and safe. She had to live another day to enjoy it. From tree to tree, around ferns and over mossy logs Jewel pressed as hard and as fast as the terrain would allow her.

When she could run no more, she hid behind the trunk of a spruce as wide as a dining table. She leaned against the tree and slid to the base, resting for only a moment. Though she knew the tree could hide her from sight, her desperate pants for oxygen were too loud and would give her away.

God, please don't let him hear me. Please don't let him find me. And please protect Officer Roberts.

Jewel didn't doubt God listened to prayers and answered them, but she wondered if maybe the mistakes she'd made and the secret she carried that had cost a life already and might cost more before this was over, kept Him from listening. Or kept the prayer from reaching Him. She didn't have the answers, but she couldn't lose hope.

Jewel sucked in oxygen, breathed in the earthy scent of the ancient forest until finally her heart rate slowed. She was still alive for the moment.

She listened. Whoever was after her didn't seem to be running—she couldn't hear any footsteps. Had he even followed?

Finally, Jewel stood. Her body hurt, but she had to keep moving. Pressing her hands into her thighs, she bent over her knees, stretching her back.

Was it Buck who had done this? She had suspected he was behind her attacks. But he was back at the house with Meral, wasn't he? This new development messed with her suspicions, and the whole reason she'd been going to town to talk to Chief Winters.

Footfalls crunched on needles.

Jewel turned and pressed her body against the tree, leaned just enough to see beyond the trunk and not expose herself. She saw no one. But still she heard him coming.

She pushed from the trunk and crept deeper into the woods. Fighting the greenery, especially since she tried to move quickly, made too much noise. If only she hadn't dropped her weapon.

How had it all gone so wrong so fast?

She could ask questions later, but first she had to survive. All she had to do was stay alive until help arrived. Had Officer Roberts been able to call for help? Was he still alive?

Her stitches hurt and her body ached afresh as though she'd come crawling from the river just this morning. She'd already tried using self-defense tactics against her attacker, but she was in pain and the man was much stronger. That didn't lend her much confidence to try again, and instead, terror gripped her.

She dropped next to another tree, catching her breath.

"Who are you? What do you want from me?" Jewel yelled, and her voice cracked with a cry from deep inside she hadn't expected. She sounded desperate and afraid— which she was, and now he knew it. She had revealed too much, proven that he had her just where he wanted her. The sound of her voice echoed through the forest, sounding eerie and like something from some twisted horror movie.

And Jewel was crumbling.

A cry broke from her throat. What was she doing except leading him right to her? Her questions didn't matter. He could hear her movement, could see where she'd been. Could have caught up with her by now if he'd wanted. Why was he torturing her?

Exhaustion and pain ate away at her resolve. She wanted to drop to the ground and wait for him to find her. After all, it was inevitable, wasn't it? Why not wait here and hang on to what energy she had left to fight?

Jewel reached deep down inside.

Get.

Up.

And run.

Hide.

She knew the area—probably better than her attacker did. Knew the woods and could use that to her advantage somehow.

She skirted the rocky outcropping and kept going. She had to make it back to the road up farther, closer to town, where her chances of running into someone and getting help would be greater. That would mean miles of running and hiking, but Jewel had spent the past two decades hiking in the woods. Participating in many of the outdoor activities her guests enjoyed, sometimes serving as a guide. She could likely outlast her pursuer.

That was if she wasn't already injured.

As she continued on, pain lashed at torn

stitches and her chest ached with every deep breath while doubts clawed at her. She came upon a hiking trail, which would make it easier for her. While she had the chance, she had to put as much distance as possible between her and the man after her. Once he found the trail, he could easily catch her.

Jewel found that even on the trail she couldn't move as fast as she'd hoped. She limped along, tried to keep from breathing so hard, but it was impossible. Her heart pounded too fast from exertion. From terror. And it all drained her energy much too quickly.

All her plans to make it to the road, to use her knowledge of the area, wouldn't work if she couldn't move, but her legs felt as if they were stuck in concrete that was quickly drying.

Pulling from what little reserve remained, Jewel limped harder and faster, pushing around the curve in the trail that led deeper into the dark canopy.

She slammed into something.

A body.

A man.

Heart palpitating, Jewel flailed away, fear stabbing through her.

He gripped her arms. Jewel screamed and fought back. Moments ago, she'd felt as if her energy was gone, but in this moment adrenaline fueled her self-defense techniques. She stunned her attacker. And freed herself from the man's grip.

Surprised, she pushed away from him, but tripped and fell on the trail. She scrambled to her feet to run, fight-or-flight hormones surging through her.

"Jewel!"

Her brain caught up with her body, cleared away the panic and confusion.

Chief Winters.

Colin.

She turned to see his approach. Then she collapsed against him.

His arms held her tight, held her up. His

words comforted her, calmed her racing heart. She was safe. How many times had she dreamed of being in his arms? Having them around her to comfort her? And how many times had she scolded herself for those forbidden thoughts? But this wasn't the same thing. She could allow herself this. And for that, she was glad.

Gathering her composure, Jewel leaned away, though he still held her. "It's not safe here. He's coming."

"Who, Jewel? Who is coming?"

"The man who has been trying to kill me. Officer Roberts—"

"Is fine. A crew is pulling him out of the vehicle even now." Pain flashed in his eyes. "I'm glad you were able to escape. I wasn't sure—"

"What are you doing here?"

Colin's broad shoulders straightened. "Looking for you. I thought it would be quicker to head you off at this trail. I figured you would come this way because you know the area."

"But what about...the man after me?" Jewel had almost said Buck, but she had too many doubts about that. Especially now. He was with Meral, and the Suburban wasn't his.

"Two officers are searching the woods, following the direction Officer Roberts thought you'd taken." He pulled her closer. "Jewel."

The way he said her name sent warmth flooding through her being. This wasn't how police officers acted with those they were sworn to help. No. Jewel recognized it for what it was.

That forbidden attraction they'd skirted for years. That Jewel had tried to ignore. With her energy focused on staying alive and solving this, the barriers protecting her heart were quickly crumbling. Her attraction to him—which went far beyond the physical—was taking hold.

Her heart pounded harder, almost making her believe she could take the risk with him.

A longing she'd forgotten threatened to pull her over and under. She squeezed her eyes shut, savoring the moment—a moment she'd never dreamed would happen. A moment she couldn't allow to continue.

It was wrong. All wrong.

She stepped from his arms and immediately missed the strength and comfort of his embrace. A chill moved in fast. But she couldn't risk the pain that she knew would follow eventually. Inevitably.

It was a matter of survival.

Colin lifted his hand to cup her cheek, but the warning look in her gaze stopped him. Conflicting emotions filled her eyes—regret and longing—and those emotions nearly did him in.

He cleared his throat and attempted to put his head and heart straight again. Should he apologize for wanting to comfort her? For wanting to be close?

He hadn't expected his own reaction. Hadn't

expected to lose control when she'd fallen into his arms, needing safety and comfort. Jewel was strong and self-sufficient and, even in this desperate crisis, he hadn't expected her need to surface like this. Or maybe he had.

Maybe he wanted her to need him.

Enough with pretense, already. He wanted to hold and comfort Jewel Caraway. And so much more. He always had. But he couldn't. From now on he should muster more control. Try harder.

Because right now he hadn't shored up his heart and mind enough. That much was clear. Already his heart was tripping and tumbling inside because she'd been attacked.

"I'm just glad I found you. Are you all right, all things considered?"

"I need to see Doc again, but I'm mostly fine. And I'm glad you found me, too." She covered her eyes for a moment, then dropped her hands. "It's not safe. He could still be out there."

"Did you see him this time?"

She shook her head and searched the woods and trail, as did Colin. "No, I was too busy running, but I heard the footfalls. I even called out to him and asked what he wanted."

Colin held his weapon, prepared to use it and end this once and for all. He almost wished the man would show himself. But with his officers combing the woods from the opposite direction, it was likely the attacker had taken off.

He used his radio to call his men. A vehicle matching the description of the black monster Suburban used in the attack had been stolen yesterday. As soon as Colin had heard the truck's description, he had known it belonged to Jim Humphrey. Good man. Made his living as a commercial fisherman. He also knew that Jim was in the hospital fighting an infection.

So far there was no sign of the truck. Colin's officers had found nothing but tracks. He could work with tracks. There were only two ways on and off this side of the mountain, and neither involved four wheels.

Colin reached for Jewel's hand. "Come on. Let me get you out of here." He paused and studied her. "Are you okay to walk?"

She nodded.

After everything she'd been through, he wasn't so sure. He gently urged her ahead of him as he watched the woods surrounding them. They had no way of knowing if her pursuer was working with someone or working alone. Better to take no chances.

If Jewel had someone like a bodyguard to stick with her all the time, maybe this would already be resolved.

But he couldn't be certain of that since an officer had been killed and another injured while watching over her. A lot of collateral damage considering the target was one small-ish middle-aged blonde woman—beautiful and strong though she was.

At the trailhead, Cobie and Adam Warren stood next to the minivan they'd purchased for the arrival of their baby. They looked ready for a hike. Colin smiled to himself. Seemed like they had plans for a bigger family. That thought stabbed him just a little. Reminded him of the big hole in his life.

Adam was wrestling a hiking pack out of the back of the van while Cobie held her baby. Colin tried to remember the baby girl's name but fell short. Was she three months old now? Time flew so fast.

When Cobie saw them, she glanced at the weapon in Colin's hand. A look of alarm flashed across her face. She tugged on Adam's sleeve. He turned and saw Colin and Jewel. For a second he froze, then dropped the pack. "Hey, Chief Winters, Jewel." His gaze jumped from Colin to Jewel. "What's going on? You run across a bear or something?"

Colin didn't want to start a panic. Nor did he want to see others hurt. "Not a bear. Two-legged creatures can be more dangerous at times. These woods aren't safe right now. Jewel was attacked and, though I think he's long gone, her attacker could still be out there."

Cobie gasped. "Oh, Jewel. Are you okay?"

"I'm fine."

But Cobie's expression said she didn't believe Jewel.

Adam's brows drew together as he directed his words to his wife. "Get in the car."

His tone was authoritative, driven by his fear and a man's need to protect his family. Cobie nodded her agreement and got into the backseat with the baby. As Cobie busied herself with putting the baby in the car seat, Adam focused on Jewel.

"Grandma Katy told me you had a scare. Got pushed into the falls. And she told me about Jed. I'm sorry about that. About all of it. I'm sorry this is happening to you, Jewel."

What did one say to that? An image of Jed's wife, Clara, flashed in Colin's mind. That's where he'd been—talking to Jed's widow—when he'd been told about the accident involving Officer Roberts and Jewel. He'd had to rush out and leave Clara with the news.

"Thank you, I guess." She flashed a weak grin and sagged against Colin.

She was in more pain than he had thought. He wanted to kick himself.

To Colin, Adam said, "I didn't realize that it wouldn't be safe out here. You've got your hands full with this investigation, huh, Chief Winters? Is there anything I can do?"

"Just keep your family safe. All of them."

"Do you know who is behind the attacks?"

"Not with any certainty."

Jewel stiffened against him, then eased back and looked him in the eyes. What was she thinking? Was she any closer to telling him what she knew?

"We'll get out of your way, then. I'll make sure the rest of the clan knows," Adam said.

The baby started crying, and Cobie glanced over her shoulder at her husband, urgent concern carved in her features.

"I wonder if it's safe for Grandma Katy to be helping at the B and B," Cobie said.

Adam shifted as though he regretted his wife's words. They could be taken wrong, sounding accusatory toward Jewel. But on the other hand, Colin wasn't sure anyone was safe anywhere near Jewel until her attacker was caught.

Colin didn't want to have that conversation in front of her, though. He scraped a hand around his jaw. "Can we talk later?"

Jewel pulled away from him and headed to Colin's Jeep, which was also parked at the trailhead.

"Does Jewel need another place to stay?" Adam asked. "I mean to throw this person off her trail? You know Grandma Katy is more than happy to have her stay at the house."

Katy Warren had already brought that up to Colin, and he had shut her down.

"You don't need to talk around me like I'm not even here," Jewel called from the Jeep. "In answer to your question, Adam, thank you, but I don't want anyone else hurt. Staying at Katy's wouldn't be any safer for me and would be more dangerous for her."

Exactly.

Adam's face paled. Did he regret making the offer? Jewel wouldn't be the first person to find a safe haven at Katy's place, but it was somehow different this time. Jewel had been brutally attacked three times now, and an officer murdered near the B and B.

No. Going to Katy's wasn't the answer.

Gunfire resounded in the woods behind them. Inside the minivan, the baby's cries grew loud and piercing. Adam dashed around to the driver's side, but then hesitated. "Are you sure there's nothing I can do to help?"

"You get your family out of here."

Adam nodded and climbed into the vehicle. Seconds later, he backed out, then drove off down the road toward Mountain Cove while Colin joined Jewel at his Jeep. He assisted her into the seat, though she tried to resist. Despite her pride, she was exhausted.

His chest hurt thinking of what she'd been through. How could he keep her safe? What could he do to comfort her now?

Frowning, Colin jogged around and climbed into the driver's side. It was then that his radio squawked. One of his officers had been struck in the head with a thick branch, but he got a shot off in self-defense. He thought he hit her, but she kept running.

"Her?" The radio at his lips, Colin jerked his gaze to Jewel, whose eyes were wide.

"Yes, chief. It was a woman."

"Keep searching." He ended the call, but his eyes never left Jewel's. "I thought you said it was a man who attacked you."

Her beautiful but tired eyes shimmered. "Whoever attacked me in the attic was a man, yes. He was much bigger and stronger than me, if that's an adequate measure. I was pressed against his chest while he was choking me, and he was solid. Nothing feminine about him."

Colin took it all in and then got on the radio

again with further instructions for his men. He needed more police in the woods to wrap this up before things escalated. He'd already put a call in to the Alaska State Troopers because of Jed's death, but it would take them time to get involved and up to speed, and things were moving fast. He didn't like any of this.

He turned on the ignition and spun the Jeep out of the trailhead. Idling next to the road, he hung on the steering wheel and looked out at the mountain and the deep greens of an old-growth forest that hid a murdering fugitive.

"I've mentioned this to you before," he said. "But I think you should consider getting out of town, just for a while, until we catch this person. I don't think there's such a thing as a safe house in Mountain Cove. Is there some place *away* from Mountain Cove that you could go? Family, friends you could visit?" Colin felt like a real heel saying the words, given what David had told him about her family. Unless Silas had a cousin or someone Colin didn't know about, the only family she had that she could turn to, lean on when times were hard, was here with her at the B and B. And, of course, her Mountain Cove friends were like family to her. But he couldn't stand the thought of another person he knew and cared about deeply getting hurt.

Especially Jewel. He didn't think she could take much more. One more incident could break her.

"If I thought for one minute that leaving Mountain Cove would end this, I would do it." Her worried gaze searched the dark woods around them.

Colin shifted in the seat and watched the woods, too. A misty fog had begun to creep through the forest, making it look ethereal and turning the woods more dangerous. He was glad he'd found Jewel when he had.

Come on. Come on out and face me, whoever you are. The both of you. At least now they knew there were two involved in the attacks against Jewel. In Jed's murder.

He needed to be out there tracking these people with his men. He hated to send them into a dangerous situation, to the front lines, when he wasn't leading the way, wasn't sharing the danger with them. He'd lost one officer and almost another one to Jewel's attackers. He feared that one by one he might lose them all.

Someone was outsmarting them. Someone was two steps ahead.

"What are you keeping from me, Jewel?"

"Nothing. I thought I knew something that could help, but I don't."

"Why don't you let me decide if it's important? That's part of my job. Help me to do my job better."

He wanted to press, to argue with her, but when she turned her eyes on him, he knew he wouldn't get another word out of her. What she was hiding was a mystery that he would have to discover on his own. What could be so important to her? He had to push down his frustration in order to be patient with the woman next to him.

He brushed her soft, ash-blond hair back, and her eyes slipped closed. What was he doing? Not very professional of him, but he couldn't seem to break away, get free from the undercurrent between them. All these years he'd kept his distance, but now he was being swept away in a river that was all woman with hazel-green eyes and a deep inner beauty he found impossible to resist. The current that was Jewel held on to him, dragging him under. How did he escape without drowning in her?

NINE

Jewel rested in the passenger seat as Colin drove her to the hospital clinic in Mountain Cove to have her injuries checked. Again. For the moment she believed she was safe, but that didn't halt her thoughts of others who had been hurt, and killed, because of her.

She searched the woods around her. Would another vehicle shoot out from the shadows and ram Colin's Jeep? Would he be the injured one this time? Or worse? Would he get killed because of her?

Lord, what do I do? Help me to do the right thing!

Head pounding, it was hard to concentrate on his cell phone conversation. But she did her best.

A woman had been shot. A woman had driven Jim Humphrey's monster Suburban into Jewel's vehicle. A woman had hunted her down when the crash hadn't killed her. Nausea roiled. The police were looking for the woman, expecting her to need medical attention, hoping the bullet had been more serious than a graze.

Jewel didn't know what to make of it. She sank deeper into the seat, letting discouragement engulf her. She'd been suspicious of Buck, but not Meral. A pang shot through her heart. A deep, wrenching ache that overshadowed all other pains.

She struggled to ignore it, to cover it up, so Colin wouldn't see her anguish. He would see right through her, and he probably already saw that she was hiding something. What was wrong with her that she wasn't strong enough, wasn't selfless enough, to tell him about her past? So what if her image, everything she'd worked to build here, would be destroyed with the truth that she was a thief?

What did her reputation matter in the light of this new revelation?

Please, God, please don't let Meral be involved.

She didn't believe it, and if there was another woman involved and not Meral, then Jewel's assailant couldn't be Buck. Or could Meral be involved, and Jewel was too naive, too blind, too unwilling to see the truth?

Jewel didn't know if she could handle yet another betrayal. And, yes, she'd felt her family had betrayed her by disowning her all those years ago. But they had believed Jewel was the betrayer, willing to leave them, to leave her inheritance behind for a man— someone without wealth and means. Someone who could never make her happy, they'd claimed.

She'd fallen for Silas because he'd filled a deep need in her that she couldn't explain. That she couldn't make her family understand.

Colin's Jeep hit a pothole and then a speed

bump, tugging her from her thoughts. Jewel rallied herself as he turned his Jeep into the clinic parking lot and assisted her out, ushering her quickly into a private room, per his request.

The nurse, Doc Harland's wife, Shana, appeared, her mouth in a flat line. "I know my husband's going to be upset seeing you in here again like this." Her eyes flicked to Colin. "You mind leaving us some privacy, good sir?"

"Fine. I'll be right outside the door." He had that demeanor about him as though he would never leave her side, but she knew he had more responsibilities than watching over her.

"Can you tell us about Officer Roberts, Shana?" she asked, believing Colin wanted to know the answer, too.

Shana's grim expression lifted a little. "He's going to be just fine. His leg is broken. Got a concussion."

Again, Shana stared at Colin. "Doc'll be in soon, Chief. We need that privacy now."

"Right outside the door, Jewel." He pinned Jewel with his gaze that told her he hadn't forgotten she was hiding something, and then he stepped into the hallway, leaving the door open. Across the hall, he leaned against the wall where he could still see Jewel and crossed his arms.

Shana closed the door on him, then turned her attention back to Jewel. "I see you pulled your stitches, hon. Doc's not going to be happy about that, I can tell you right now."

Jewel sat on the examination table and let Shana jabber on while she took Jewel's blood pressure. "Your BP's a little high, too, but that's understandable given the circumstances. You stay right here, and Doc will be in with you in a moment."

She left Jewel alone. Jewel closed her eyes. Quiet. That was all she needed. A moment alone. Jewel thought about Colin's words. Maybe he was right. She would have to leave Mountain Cove. Maybe even Alaska. But for how long? What if she left for good?

She could sell the B and B and live off that money. She'd had a few offers over the years. And somehow she had to figure out how to rid herself of the diamond—the very reason someone was trying to kill her. Or was it? With these new developments, she wasn't so sure anymore.

Doc Harland entered the room much too soon. Jewel wasn't up to his friendly conversation. She smiled and nodded the best she could, but she probably reacted more like a zombie to him. She hoped he understood.

When he examined her gash, she winced and let out a soft cry. Then he restitched it in places. "Sorry, if I hurt you. You sure don't need anything more to add to your pain."

When he was done, he went to the small sink and washed his hands.

"Despite your pain and torn sutures, I'd say you're healing up nicely. But it looks like you have some new bruises from the seat belt that likely saved your life."

Jewel could only nod. She had no energy

for speech. No words of wisdom for anyone, especially herself.

The good doctor dropped his stethoscope and stared at Jewel until she focused on him. He had her attention now like he wanted. "Seems to me what hurts the most is in here." He pointed at her head. "And here." And then to her heart. "And I'm very sorry, but I don't have a salve for that."

Jewel appreciated that he paid attention and saw through her physical pain to what was going on inside. "Even if you had medicine, it wouldn't work until this is over, if it ever could work." *And if it ever ends.* Especially if Meral was involved.

Jewel was beginning to doubt it would end until she was dead.

His left brow arched. "I'm sure you're right. My only advice to you is to stick close to the Lord. I know you're a praying woman, Jewel. This is a trying time for you, but never doubt God loves you. Easy enough to see that He sent you a protector. So you only need to stay close to that man standing out in the hallway who cares deeply for you. But by the looks of things, he isn't going to give you much choice. The good news is that he'll protect you and maybe offer the healing touch to your heart that you need, as well."

The look in Doc Harland's eyes and the deeper meaning behind his words warmed her cheeks. At that moment, Jewel knew that a fortyish widow could blush as easily as a young twentysomething. But she didn't want anyone to get the wrong idea.

"There's nothing between us." The words rushed out.

Doc nodded, his expression reflecting that he didn't believe her. When he was done, he opened the door. "She's all yours, Chief."

Colin stepped into the room. He hadn't left even to check on Officer Roberts? He squeezed Doc's arm. "Thank you for taking care of my officer, Doc. I can't lose another person to this. And thanks for looking after Jewel, paying her special attention."

"Jewel is a special woman, and don't you forget it." Doc Harland winked at Jewel. "Matt Roberts will be fine. His family's here. They'll get him back to you as good as new."

Colin smiled as the doctor left, then he shut the door behind him before pinning her with those stark blue eyes that didn't miss a detail. That could practically read her mind. She tried her best to shutter away her pain. And her secret.

"I don't want to keep you," she said. "I know you have a job to do."

"You mean protecting Mountain Cove?"

"That's the job, yes."

"I can guarantee you that everyone wants Mountain Cove police to find the person who killed Jed Turner. To stop this person before someone else gets hurt or killed. This case is my priority. Nothing is more important to me."

"And I'm…in the center of that."

"You're the target, yes. You're my priority." Of course this would be his priority. But there was something else, some anguish winding through his gaze that told her this was personal. She averted her own. She didn't want that from him.

That's a lie...

Jewel had never been good at lying to herself. Okay, so maybe she would admit that she did want that from him, but what difference did it make? Wanting and having were two different things. She'd have to work harder to keep her distance from him. That was all. Yet the pain in his eyes reflected back to her and made her realize that she could hardly stand to hurt him any more than she wanted to risk her own heart.

He had read well enough she was hiding something, and that had hurt him.

Hurt him.

Oh, Colin, if you knew the truth...

She wanted to tell him everything. Her doubts and fears, but she'd already decided that telling him she'd stolen something years ago, even if it was from her family during a crisis, would dim the light she saw in his eyes.

As an officer of the law, he would think less of her. How could he not?

And Jewel couldn't stand the thought of that. Since Buck didn't seem to be her attacker, that meant the attacks had nothing to do with the stolen diamond, so she wasn't hurting anyone by keeping her secret.

She remembered when Colin had found her today. She'd fallen against him in relief. Gone right into his arms, to an emotional place she'd never been before with him. She thought back to years gone by and realized that he'd been there for her so many times— just in the background, just on the edge, but he'd been there watching over her all the same.

"I'm taking you to the B and B now, but you should know, as long as you insist on staying there, I'm going to be there to watch over you myself. I'll switch out with my officers and take the night watch. Nothing is more important than catching these guys and keeping you safe."

"That would be like working two jobs. You can't be my personal bodyguard and run the police department."

"You might be surprised at what I'm capable of."

Meral came rushing into the exam room followed by Buck. "Oh, Jewel, are you okay?"

Surprise and relief whooshed through Jewel as Meral hugged her, careful to avoid her back where the stitches had been repaired. Holding her sister, Jewel tried to determine if Meral had suffered an injury, even a graze from a bullet. The officer hadn't been certain his shot had found a target, so Jewel couldn't be certain about anything either.

Still, Jewel desperately wanted to believe that Meral could not be the woman in the monster Suburban who had rammed her vehicle off the road. Who had hunted for her in the woods to kill her. Behind her, Buck appeared concerned for Jewel's well-being, as well.

In her peripheral vision, Jewel saw Colin stand back and study them. Scrutinize them as though he suspected them. Why? What reason could he have? He didn't know Jewel's secret. Then again, as chief of police, he was probably suspicious of everyone.

Meral released Jewel and brushed away her hair, like any loving sister. Not like a woman who had only appeared in her life to search for a small fortune or to stab her sister in the back. How could Jewel have ever suspected Meral?

Shame threatened to undo her, but she buried it. Fought to rise above all that pulled her down.

"Jewel, listen, Buck has come up with a great idea." Meral looked at Colin. "I'm glad you're here, too, Chief Winters. I think this could solve all your problems."

Colin stiffened. Dropped his arms to his side.

"We're chartering a boat to explore southeast Alaska. The Inside Passage."

Jewel's stomach lurched. "But...you're leaving already? How would that solve any problems? I don't want you to go yet."

A grin slipped on to Meral's lips. "You're coming with us."

"But I have a business to run and can't abandon my guests."

"You can't stay in that house either. It's dangerous for your guests, too. Wouldn't you agree, Chief Winters?" Meral directed her question to Colin.

His lips pursed. "I can't argue with that."

Jewel wasn't sure that leaving would make her any safer. But it might draw out her attacker and bring things to an end. It would mean she wasn't just waiting around for another attack. That she was being proactive.

She pursed her lips.

"Don't worry, Jewel. You can leave," Meral continued. "I spent this afternoon talking to your employees, Jan and Frances, and to Tracy and Katy. You've thoroughly trained them to pitch in as needed. I think you can take a few days off, a week or even two, for your own vacation. That would get you away from this insanity. Nothing can happen to you on a boat with just your family."

Meral stepped away from Jewel and into Buck's arms. "Besides, we've already chartered the boat. We leave in two days."

Jewel pushed her face into her hands. She couldn't take all the eyes on her. Couldn't take the pressure of having to make such a hasty decision in the face of everything that was happening. But Meral was right. She couldn't keep her B and B open if she stayed there. She couldn't expect the Mountain Cove police officers to continue putting themselves in harm's way to protect her either.

And she had the feeling that Meral would go with or without her. Jewel couldn't let her time with Meral slip away so fast. Colin had suggested she leave, get out of town, and this could be the answer. She could also keep an eye on Buck for Meral's sake. She still had the feeling Buck was using Meral.

As if she could protect Meral, given she'd done such a great job protecting herself.

Why hadn't Meral seen through Buck before she'd married him? But then, maybe that was how Jewel's parents had felt when Jewel had chosen Silas. Except they had been wrong about him.

Could she be wrong about Buck?

She looked up. Everyone was still waiting. "I need to think about it."

"You have a day. We'll need time to get you ready for the trip. But I really don't see you have a choice," Meral said.

Jewel locked eyes with Colin. Why wasn't he saying anything? But he'd already told her to go. Maybe that was enough.

It would mean she couldn't stick close to the man who wanted to protect her, like Doc Harland said. Doc seemed to believe God had put Colin in her life to protect her, but what happened now if she left that protection behind in search of a safe place?

* * *

Colin sat in the chair across the antique mahogany desk from Mayor Judy Conroy. A driven woman in her early fifties, she liked to dress the part of a politician. Had a stylish hairdo and ordered her suits from some fancy place out of Seattle. No matter the weather, she would always wear matching pumps. And she liked to control and intimidate.

But she hadn't called him into her office today. No. He'd come here of his own volition, needing to detail his plans and ask permission, something he never liked to do. Especially since he could see in her eyes she had plans of her own—to berate Colin.

She sucked in a breath, opened her mouth and her cell buzzed on her desk. After a glance down she released that breath, then looked back at him. "Sorry, Chief. Gotta take this. It won't be but a second."

"No problem."

She was on the cell before he responded. He released a pent-up sigh and tried to calm himself. The call would give him a few seconds, hopefully minutes, to regain his nerve. He tapped his fingers on her desk while he waited for her to end the phone call.

Where did he start? How did he present his case?

She jabbered on with her niece, Taney Westmore, while Colin tried to ignore the conversation. He got up to pace the room. What he wanted to do was put his fist through the wall. He'd never been so frustrated.

He'd been the one to suggest that Jewel get out of town, and now he was incredibly bothered by the idea that she was taking his advice. He should have considered that if Jewel left town, Buck would be with her because Meral would be with her.

But Colin hadn't thought that through very well. "Idiot," he mumbled under his breath with a quick glance at the mayor. Wouldn't do for her to think he had just called her a name.

No, he needed her in a good mood. Problem was he had been the one to put her in a perpetually bad mood lately. Now add that one of his officers had been murdered and another one injured, and the mayor would likely tear into him before he got a word in edgewise.

The pressure was on and seemed to be measured by the pounding in his head.

Finally, he plopped in the chair again, afraid that if he kept pacing he would, in fact, put a fist through the wall in the mayor's office, and that wouldn't go over well. He noticed a Holy Bible sitting at the corner of her desk and took a minute to seek some guidance. Closing his eyes, he drew in a calming breath.

God, I could use a little help here. I'm in a serious predicament. Help me to do what needs to be done. Help me get Jed's killer before he kills again. Help me keep Jewel safe.

"Sleeping on the job?"

He opened his eyes to see that she had ended her call. "No, just saying a little prayer."

"That bad, huh?" Her brows drew together. "Sorry about the call, but I had to take it."

"No problem." He should ask if everything

was all right with Taney, but that would send them down a road he didn't want to go right now.

She pressed her elbows on her desk and rested her chin in her clasped hands. "What can I do for you?"

Colin could see it in her eyes. That was a trick question—she was waiting for him to say something she could criticize. Everything he was about to say went against his personal policy, his resolve to act only on the cold hard facts. He pulled in a breath.

Here goes nothing or everything.

"I have a possible lead on Jed's murder and on who attacked Jewel Caraway."

"Is that so?"

"But I need to follow it up."

The mayor dropped her hands and pushed from the chair. Now she was the one pacing. Building up steam to blast him with, no doubt. "And by follow up you mean what?"

Colin scratched his chin. Explaining this wasn't going to be easy. "This all started when Jewel's sister and husband, Meral and Buck, arrived. I checked on him, but he came back clean. He's some sort of import and export consultant."

"What aren't you telling me, Colin?" Now the mayor had gone personal with his name. Never a good sign.

"I need to leave. Jewel, Meral and Buck are going on a short cruise, a tour of Alaska. A week or two. I need to be there with her to protect her and to find out if Buck is the man who killed Jed."

There. He'd spoken his mind.

"It would mean you wouldn't be here for Jed's funeral."

He nodded, hating the timing. "What's more important? Getting Jed's killer or attending his funeral?"

"What reason have you got to suspect Buck? Give me something, anything, and I'll think about it."

"A feeling."

Her eyes blazed. *Here it comes.*

"Let me get this straight. You want to go off on what amounts to a vacation while we have a murderer out there based on a feeling?"

"No. It's not like that." He knew the man from somewhere, and though he couldn't remember the circumstances, Buck gave him a bad feeling. A very bad feeling.

"Oh, I think it is. You're infatuated with Jewel. Let me make myself perfectly clear, Chief Winters. You think that you're under pressure now? Let me assure you that I am under tremendous pressure as this town's mayor. People want to know why this is happening to our town. And what about Jed's family? How do you think they are going to see your actions? His wife, his kids and the town want to know why someone—a fine and upstanding officer of the law, no less— has been murdered. Not long ago others were murdered. Businesses burned down. People were scared to come out of their houses or even go to the dentist because maybe a bomb would blow up while they were sitting in the chair. You took far too long to solve those cases, and this one is still open, with a killer still free. So, no, I can't let you go on a trip with your precious Jewel based on nothing more than a feeling."

The mayor's face was red. Though he'd been the object of her complaints before, this was the worst dressing-down he'd ever gotten. He supposed he'd given her reason enough.

"You see, here's the thing." He stood to give himself the edge. "The reason I didn't solve those cases quicker is because I refused to listen to my gut. I refused to go on anything but the facts. But the hard truth of it is that solving an investigation takes a good measure of both gut feeling and facts. Not one or the other but both working together. I have to ask myself what kind of police chief doesn't listen to his gut instincts? A poor one. And I'm sorry that I didn't realize that sooner. Now, please, let me follow my instincts on this." He was so tired of second-guessing himself, and for the first time in a long time, he believed he was doing the right thing. Now if only he could convince the mayor.

She took a seat and sighed. "Give me something. You have to give me something solid, Chief. What are people going to say?"

As if he cared anymore. Colin detested politics, but there was no getting around them. "Even if I give you a reason, a solid lead or evidence, they're going to talk. They're going to spin this trip in a negative light."

"True." The mayor sagged in her seat and slowly shook her head. "I'm sorry. I can't let you go. You're going to have to figure out how to solve this case here in Mountain Cove while working in your capacity as chief of police, not gallivanting around the Inside Passage with the woman everyone knows you love."

Love? Colin narrowed his eyes. He was about to open his mouth to speak, but she beat him to it.

"I'm sorry, Colin. I shouldn't have said that.

It's none of my business. If you want to protect her, then get this guy, but you'll have to do it while remaining in your jurisdiction and functioning in your full capacity as the Mountain Cove chief of police. If you need a presence there with Jewel, send one of your officers, but I can't let you go yourself."

There was that image of his fist slamming into the wall again. Wasn't she listening? The only way to get the bad guy was to go with Jewel. Nobody else could do this. It had to be Colin. He was the one with the gut feeling. He didn't dare risk another one of his men or send them into danger on instincts alone.

As for gathering evidence against Buck, he'd contacted a friend, the forensic artist from Juneau that Mountain Cove sometimes used, to take some years and pounds off Buck's photo to help Colin figure out why he recognized him. But it wasn't under the official umbrella of police business, so it might not come in time. He couldn't tell her about that—it might be a dead end.

I have no choice.

His next words pained him, weakened his legs, but he had to do it.

"Okay, then, maybe I care about Jewel more than I should, but this isn't about that. It comes down to the fact that I couldn't live with myself if something happened to her, especially when I know how to prevent it."

He'd already experienced losing someone he loved, but he wouldn't tell the mayor about that. He'd already said too much. He didn't need to explain himself, but maybe part of him hoped if he showed a little more of himself, she would be more understanding.

It all flooded back and swirled through his mind in a quick second before he could blink and formulate his next words.

He'd planned to propose, but Katelyn had been murdered and all because she had witnessed a crime. He hadn't been able to arrest the man without her testimony, and afterward the charges brought against the man for her murder had been dismissed because of shoddy DNA and the killer's airtight alibi. Colin had failed Katelyn miserably. That was why from then on he'd made sure he only worked off the facts. He'd made sure he wasn't emotionally involved with a woman he needed to protect.

But that couldn't be helped this time. And he wouldn't fail Jewel. He wouldn't let himself get any more involved with her either. He'd keep it professional. Wouldn't let his heart even dip a toe in the water, but he would protect her if it was the last thing he did.

Another problem drilled through the tension. He hadn't been invited to go with Jewel, but the boat left this afternoon and he had to move quickly. He'd already deliberated far too long about how to handle this. And now it came down to worst-case scenarios. Had he convinced the mayor? Or not?

Her eyes softened, but it wasn't enough. That much he could see. "Colin...I..." She blew out a breath, clearly unsettled by his words. "I'm sorry."

"You'll have my resignation letter on your desk by the end of the day."

TEN

The privately chartered yacht, *The Alabaster Sky*, waited at the dock for the passengers to board. From the outside, Jewel could already see the yacht was modern and luxurious, and she guessed between sixty and seventy feet long. Though it had only been chartered for the trip, it had to have cost a small fortune. A year's salary for some. She'd forgotten what real wealth could buy. When she'd offered to pay for her portion of the trip, Meral had reassured her it was all taken care of.

Next to her, Buck and Meral unloaded the rest of the luggage from the cab.

Jewel's palms slicked. Nausea swelled. Was she making a mistake?

Colin had told her to get out of town so she

would be safe. So she could escape her attackers before they succeeded in killing her. But Colin had had no idea that she suspected Buck when he'd said the words. And even though it didn't seem possible that he was involved in the incident that totaled her vehicle and injured an officer, her suspicions had crept back in with a vengeance and she couldn't let go of them.

With the Krizan Diamond burning a hole in the bag she shouldered much too protectively, she would find out sooner rather than later. She'd managed to sneak up to the attic again and pull the rock from its hiding place. She couldn't bring herself to leave it there to be stolen, if that's why her attacker had been in the attic—to search for the diamond.

She should have put it in a safe-deposit box, but she hadn't been able to break away from Meral and Buck. And to ask them to stop at the bank for her to take care of business would have been futile. They would have marched right in with her. Heard her say she wanted a safe-deposit box. Then the questions would have come. It was a small town, and others would see and talk.

She was trapped.

It was all so awkward.

And if Buck was after the diamond, he would know that Jewel suspected his motives. He might even hope that she would bring it with her to keep it safe or, out of desperation, to lure out her attacker. In that case, he might look for it on the boat.

But was she thinking clearly about this? It was hard to know with the attempts on her life holding her mind hostage and the likely reason weighing heavy in her pack.

She was some kind of crazy to attempt this.

Besides, if Buck really was involved, and he really was after the diamond, then putting it in a safe-deposit box in the bank like any normal person would virtually guarantee Jewel's death. Kill Jewel and the items in her safe-deposit box would go to Meral, who was named in Jewel's will after she'd lost Silas, a fact she'd shared with her sister shortly after her arrival in Mountain Cove. That had been her way to make sure the diamond went back to her family. Maybe that was why her attacker had tried to kill her. He thought it was stored safely away—whoever he was. A man and a woman working together.

Meral and Buck.

Her heart sank.

Jewel hung her head. *I don't know, I just don't know anymore.*

She didn't want to believe it of Meral. Yet doubt suffused her. This trip had been Buck's idea, just like coming to Mountain Cove.

Her pulse raced and jumped. Had agreeing to this been a wise decision?

What did it matter? If there was any chance that Meral was not involved, then Jewel had to be with Meral to spend time with her and protect her, if she could.

Meral set Jewel's bag next to her feet. "You okay?"

The question pulled Jewel back to the present. "Sure."

"You don't look okay." Meral eyed her.

Buck paid the cab driver.

"I'll be fine, Meral." Jewel gave her sister a quick hug.

Buck's dark eyes and fake smile landed on Jewel. "Let's go."

Jewel released her sister to Buck. Two men and a woman appeared on the yacht and came down the gangplank to greet them.

The older of the crew members thrust out his hand and shook Buck's in a hearty greeting, then turned his attention to Meral and Jewel. "Good afternoon, ladies. I'm captain of *The Alabaster Sky*. You can call me Mike or Captain Mike, whatever you prefer. This is Gary, our deckhand, and Stella, your hostess and steward. And Mack's the chef, but he's in the kitchen preparing your meal for this evening."

Private and chartered yachts and cruise ships were a familiar sight in southeast Alaska, and some even stopped in Mountain Cove. But Jewel had never met any of the staff that operated those vessels, so it was strange when a sense of recognition pricked her at Stella's smile. Gary had a familiar face, too, but maybe they each just had one of those faces that everyone thought they knew. Jewel was sure she'd never met either of them.

Buck grinned. He gave the captain's hand a second good, hard shake. "Captain Mike here is one of the best. Decades of experience and he knows all the sweet spots in the channels, full of isolated and undisturbed nature. This is going to be the adventure of a lifetime. I'm going fishing for the catch of my life."

With his last words, Buck's eyes locked with Jewel's.

"Let's get the adventure of a lifetime going," Stella said, smiling sweetly.

Jewel bent to lift her luggage.

"Oh, no, I'll get that," Stella said. "All part of the package."

The crew gathered up their bags and lugged everything up the gangplank. Jewel stared at the luxury cruiser yacht. Arm in arm, Meral and Buck followed the crew.

"Come on, Jewel!" Meral yelled over her shoulder.

Jewel's throat went dry.

What am I doing? Was she getting on this boat with a killer? Jewel felt like the absolute worst kind of traitor to think these awful thoughts. Meral was giddy with excitement and looked much younger than her years. Jewel should be happy for Meral.

Instead, she felt seasick and she hadn't even boarded the yacht. She was leaving her self-proclaimed protector behind. Yet, she wasn't truly alone.

God had been her refuge and would continue to be. And she had let Colin go, what small part of him she had held on to in her heart. She had no right to think about him or hang on to him when she simply wasn't willing to risk that much.

Tears threatened, burning her eyes and throat. But she focused on the yacht in front of her and this new adventure, praying it wouldn't be deadly. A piece of her hoped this trip would force the truth—good or bad—to come out and she would at last be free from the threats on her life.

Finally, Jewel followed her sister and Buck onto the boat, where Stella, carrying Jewel's luggage, showed Jewel to her quarters. Jewel trailed her, containing her gasp at the spacious room, though she shouldn't have been surprised. Stella set Jewel's luggage next to the king-size bed covered in an elegant seashell spread in shades of teal.

Stella held out her hand. "Can I take your bag?"

Jewel tugged it closer. "Uh, no. I can unpack my things, thank you." She forced a smile and tried to relax.

Stella never lost her bright smile and went around the expansive stateroom explaining all the amenities like a well-practiced tour guide. The woman was in her mid to late twenties, slender and athletic, and a full head taller than Jewel. Her warm brown hair was secured in a ponytail and hidden beneath a white cap.

She stood at another door. "And in here, you'll find a full bath with a large shower."

"Thank you, Stella. I appreciate you showing me around."

She clasped her hands in front of her. "Will there be anything else?"

"No. I'll unpack my things and freshen up for dinner. When do we leave?"

"In half an hour or less, when everyone is settled in."

Once alone, Jewel paced the luxurious room, feeling completely out of place, though she'd grown up in an old-money family and shouldn't have felt uncomfortable. Had she been away from it all so long that she felt out of place here?

But one thing was certain. Meral hadn't been disinherited—at least not yet—if chartering a private yacht for a few days was nothing to her. Or maybe Buck, who could have his own money, had paid for it. Jewel didn't know a thing about him, and maybe that was what disturbed her the most.

But after the life Jewel had lived in Alaska, which consisted of hard work to earn a living and make ends meet, Jewel found this kind of wealth difficult to handle.

It didn't feel right. She didn't belong here. Jewel grabbed her bag. Forget her luggage. Easier to sneak off without it. Loathing herself for her indecision, loathing herself for doing this to Meral, she stepped into the hallway. Quietly, she shut the door behind her.

Then froze.

Buck stood at the other end of the hall in a wide stance.

He didn't smile or speak.

He just stood there and stared at her. She should move or say something, but she felt the urge to turn and run. The skin on the back of her neck crawled, and she had the keen sense that Buck would react like a rabid dog at the prospect of a chase.

No. She couldn't run.

Meral stepped from a room and leaned against Buck, who hugged her to him, but his eyes were slow to pull from Jewel.

After planting a kiss on his lips, Meral laughed and pulled away, only now noticing Jewel. Her smile dropped. "Jewel, what's the matter? Why don't you get settled in your room?"

Oh, how did Jewel tell her sister there was no way she could stay? Her heart crashed against her ribcage.

Suddenly, Meral's eyes focused beyond Jewel's shoulder. Buck's eyes narrowed.

"I finally made it," a familiar voice spoke from behind. "Thought I was going to miss the boat."

Colin.

Jewel whipped around. Chief Colin Winters confidently strode toward her. Her heart bounced around at the sight of him. At the relief that he was here. He was dressed in a casual polo shirt and jeans and carried a duffel bag and jacket slung over his shoulder. He'd always looked good—authoritative and powerful—in his police attire. But now Colin was not the law. He was just a man and not just any man. A slow hum started in her stomach. She couldn't find the words to greet him.

"What are you doing here?" Buck asked.

Jewel almost opened her mouth to ask the same question, but without missing a beat, Colin answered, "Jewel invited me. Didn't she tell you?"

Buck laughed.

Meral gave him a jab. "Shush. Well, we're delighted to have you, Chief Winters."

"Colin. It's just Colin. I'm not on duty now."

A million questions ran through Jewel's mind. Like how had he swung this? Would Meral and Buck make him pay for the ride? Would that clean out the man's savings? But it didn't matter. Jewel wanted to run into his arms like Meral had done with Buck, but she and Colin weren't in that kind of relationship.

There was a question in his eyes.

Would she play along?

Yes. Yes, she would definitely play along.

"I'm sorry, Meral. With everything going on, it must have slipped my mind. But remember, he promised not to leave my side until this was over."

Meral giggled. "Yes, but the whole purpose of the trip was to keep you safe. You don't need a protector here. Uh-huh. I'm on to you two. You can't fool me for a minute."

Jewel opened her mouth to correct Meral, but hesitated. She wasn't sure what to say to Meral's innuendos. Protesting that there was nothing between them would make things even more awkward. She had no idea how to act or respond.

Meral filled the silence with her exuberance. "But this will be so much fun!"

Could Meral be so incredibly clueless?

Stella appeared and showed Colin to his quarters down the hall. Jewel slipped back into her own room and let the bag slide to the floor. She was staying after all.

Now, where could she hide a diamond worth a fortune?

* * *

They traveled from Mountain Cove, heading north a short distance to stop and anchor for the night at an isolated cove off a nearby island. From there, they could watch for whales and sea lions. Maybe do some fishing. Buck claimed he was looking forward to catching halibut with Colin.

At dinner that evening they were served on the deck outside, under the stars. This time of year in southeast Alaska, the sunrise and sunset, as well as the weather, was more like that in the lower forty-eight.

A gorgeous night in a beautiful, secluded cove. Colin had to fight hard against relaxing into this dream vacation. It would be easy to imagine or pretend he was here with Jewel for personal reasons. That could be dangerous on too many levels, and if his hunch was right, cost their lives. That sober reminder kept him focused and on task.

Meral and Buck laughed, and the conversation was stimulating, but never veering too close to personal topics for any in the group, which was just as well. Colin didn't want to answer questions about his life before Mountain Cove. Interesting to think they each had secrets—pasts they weren't willing to share. Yet the conversation never ran out. Buck was intelligent and an eloquent conversationalist, knowledgeable on more subjects than most people Colin had met. Which would make him a great con artist.

Buck grinned at Meral, his gaze flicking to Jewel and back.

A memory flashed. Something at the edge of Colin's mind. Why couldn't he remember? He'd gone through photos of past investigations and had come up empty.

It would come to him, but would it come too late?

Jewel excused herself and left the table, promising to return in a minute or two.

While she was gone, Buck turned his attention on Colin.

"So tell me, Chief...er...Colin. How did you get away from town with a killer on the loose?" Buck asked. "I mean, Jewel's here with us and obviously safe, so why would they let you leave in the middle of an investigation? It's hard to imagine that the police chief would be assigned to bodyguard duty in these circumstances. Unless…oh, I know—" Buck snapped his fingers "—you assigned yourself."

Have a care now how you answer. How much should he reveal?

Meral put her hand on Buck's cheek and forced his face toward hers. "Now you leave him alone," she said, but Buck's gaze never left Colin's. It was clear the man had not been happy to see him. Didn't want him on the boat. Why not?

"The mayor trusts me to follow my instincts," Colin said. That should be answer enough.

And then a slight curve came to Buck's lips—that smirk again. A challenge?

A tingling sensation crawled over Colin. He knew that smirk. What good was he if he couldn't remember?

He'd been right to resign from his job and come, of that he had no doubt. When he'd walked into the hall and caught that feral look in Buck's eyes as the man had looked at Jewel, he'd known.

Maybe on this yacht Jewel would finally tell him what she hadn't been willing to share so far. But he had to keep his heart out of it and use his head at all times.

He thought back to the cell phone call he'd received from the mayor right before boarding the yacht.

"Chief Winters, I don't accept your resignation."

"Excuse me?"

"I know what I said in the heat of the moment, but despite our recent troubles, I don't believe we'll find a better man for the job. So I'm going to give you the time away you need. I'll hold down the fort while you're gone, so to speak. I'm not sure whether to tell the boys you're on a covert mission or that you've taken some time, but just do me one favor."

"What's that?"

"Get this guy, Colin. You return with our murderer, and that'll save me a lot of explaining."

Jewel returned, and they finished the rest of the dinner talking about the Alaska scenery.

Stella approached the table and removed their plates, then Meral and Buck excused themselves to go for a walk on the deck.

Colin was left alone with Jewel at the table. A candle burned in the center. While planning ahead for this adventure, he'd known he would be thrust into a romantic setting, and this certainly fit the bill. He just had to remember that it was set against a murderous backdrop. Still, no matter how he mentally prepared himself, he hadn't fully grasped how much being here with Jewel would impact him. Jewel, with her ash-blond hair and striking, lovely hazel-green eyes that shined with a soft inner light had Colin struggling to breathe.

Being here with her like this without reaching over and grabbing her hand, touching her face, reaching out to hold her, might be the most difficult thing Colin had ever done. Jewel was so beautiful. If they let their hearts have free rein, she could be all he wanted. He never doubted that.

But danger lurked on the yacht with them. Whether that danger had anything to do with Jewel's attacker remained to be seen. But he could feel it, sense it. Now that he let himself feel again and listen to his instincts, that danger reading was off the charts.

Focus, man. Focus.

He cleared his throat and tensed, forcing a harsh expression that felt completely wrong for the moment. "Now that we have a moment alone, I want to thank you for covering for me. I meant to…well…I meant to talk to you first and get myself an actual invitation."

"I guess I should have invited you. I didn't

think it was appropriate. Or that you could leave your job."

Oh yeah. That. If she only knew.

"So why *did* you come?" In her eyes, he thought he saw that she was searching, wanting to know a deeper truth. One he couldn't admit.

"The reason you gave them. I'm not leaving your side until this is over."

"But how will you catch my attacker if you're on the boat with me?" An odd look washed over Jewel's face, and the moonlit sparkle in her eyes vanished.

"I thought getting away was the answer, but as soon as you made plans to leave, I realized that your attacker might follow you. I'm going to keep you safe just like I said."

She scoffed a laugh like she didn't believe him. Didn't trust his ability to protect her.

Or was it that she knew he didn't have all the information?

"What haven't you told me, Jewel?"

"I haven't told you thank you." She smiled. "I'm glad you're here."

Jewel stood and moved to the rail to look out over the waters of the Inside Passage. He followed her and leaned against the railing next to her.

The only thing to make the moment more perfect would be to see the aurora borealis.

Yeah. This was definitely the hardest thing he'd ever done. Beautiful woman at his side on an amazing Alaskan cruise, and his senses were heightened to her every breath, her every look, her every smile, her shimmering gaze. But not fifty feet from them stood a dangerous man. Colin didn't want Buck to be her attacker. But he also wanted to catch the person who'd tried to kill Jewel and had succeeded in killing Jed.

He watched Buck with Meral in the shadows at the bow. What a strangely precarious situation he was in now. Here to protect Jewel from a killer while he protected himself from Jewel.

God, You have a way of testing us, putting us through trials to make us stronger. But right now I feel weak. And maybe that's Your plan. But doesn't mean I have to like it.

And he didn't like this familiar feeling. Like he was right back where he had been before, trying and failing to protect a woman he cared deeply about from a man set on killing her.

And this time, they were all together like one happy family on the boat ride of their lives.

ELEVEN

The room was spacious, but Jewel still felt trapped. Jewel sat up in bed against a couple of pillows and held another wrapped in her arms as if it could protect her.

How was she supposed to get any rest on this opulent yacht in this crazy situation, which was both dangerous and awkward? It was as if she had jumped from the proverbial frying pan right into the fire. And not only where her life was concerned. When Colin had showed up just in time to fend off the strange vibes coming from Buck, her heart had been instantly in jeopardy.

More pressing was her physical being—her life. Every creak of the boat, every sound, had her on edge. She couldn't possibly close her eyes, much less sleep.

Colin was down the hall in his room, but he might as well be back in Mountain Cove for all the good his presence would do if she were attacked. She still ached from the previous attempts on her life.

Oh, God, what was I thinking to do this? Is Buck the man who attacked me or not? She couldn't decide. Her imagination was working overtime.

Except. An image projected across her mind.

The way Buck had stood there in the hallway, his wide stance. Hadn't she seen that stance before—above the water on the ledge?

Jewel climbed from bed. Standing, expanding her lungs would help her catch her breath. But after several tries she realized she was hyperventilating. Breathing too hard and fast and getting too much oxygen. She'd never experienced this before. Her life had never been pushed so close to the edge. Though she didn't have a paper bag to breathe into, she could use her hands. She cupped her palms over her mouth to balance out the oxygen with carbon dioxide.

A sound from the hall drew her attention. She stood still, listening.

Footfalls?

Her doorknob twisted quietly.

Though her door was locked, the fact someone wanted in still terrified her.

Lord, help me!

Jewel ran to the table next to the bed and grabbed the gun she'd brought on board with her bag. She wrapped her hand around the cool plastic of her 9-millimeter pistol, hoping it would reassure her. But any reassurance was lost with the thought that her attacker stood on the other side of the door.

Trying to get into her room.

But she must face him head-on this time. She hurried to the door that had no peephole. "Who's there?"

She might as well face him and get it over with.

"It's me." Colin's voice was soft.

What is he doing here? She cracked the door. "You scared me to death."

"You look like you're still alive to me."

"What are you doing?"

"I'm sorry to scare you. I was checking your door to make sure it was locked. Now get some sleep."

She swung the door a little wider and stuck out her head to look in the hallway. "I'm having some trouble with that."

"That's understandable after what you've been through. But I told you I was here to protect you, so that's what I'm doing. It's no different than me staying at your B and B, if you want to think of it that way." He cracked a half grin, then his gaze dropped. "I'm glad it's not your policy to shoot first and ask questions later. I'm glad, too, that you brought your own protection."

She lifted the Glock, trusting the feel of it in her hands. "Don't worry. I know how to use it. I can take care of myself." But she wasn't feeling secure. Wasn't feeling it at all. The thought of facing off with another human being and shooting him wasn't appealing in the least, even if it meant putting an end to her attacks.

Jewel opened her door wider. "Come in, so we don't wake the others."

He hesitated, something raw anchored in those starkly blue eyes, then shook his head. He wasn't coming into her room. He either didn't trust himself or he didn't trust her.

Her heart did a somersault. He was rugged and handsome and a protector all wrapped up in one way-too-appealing package. And he'd assigned himself as her personal bodyguard. Something inside told her he wouldn't be here if it wasn't much more than police business. If it wasn't personal to him.

"So what? Are you planning to stand guard outside my room all night, then?"

"If that's what it takes."

The disquiet in his eyes tugged at her heart. She reached out and pressed her hand against his cheek, feeling the stubble there. A current surged up her arm. Mistake. It had been a mistake to reach out, but she couldn't seem to pull her hand back. She was enjoying that slow hum in her belly entirely too much.

"I don't know how you can watch over me 24/7," she said. The hitch in her voice told more than she wanted to reveal. "You have to rest, too."

He stepped back, forcing Jewel to drop her hand. His move had been intentional, and she was grateful. What had she been thinking? She couldn't think at all when next to him anymore.

"No one camped outside my room at the B and B, and I'm safer here than I was there."

"That why you brought the gun? You believe you're safe now?" It was rhetorical. He was making a point. "Good night, Jewel."

"Good night." She closed the door and pressed her back against it.

He hadn't expected Jewel to answer, because he'd seen the truth in her eyes and in her actions. They were both dancing around that truth, because Jewel was unwilling to tell him. But now he had confirmation from her that he'd been right to come. He'd been right to listen to his gut if even Jewel thought she wasn't safe on this yacht with her sister and brother-in-law.

And he knew to be even more vigilant. He kept his door open. Sat in a chair and watched the hallway, his eyes on Jewel's door.

Come on, Buck, make a move. Make a move while I'm here so I can catch you and put you away. So I can stop the attack and prevent more. Make a move so we can all get back to our lives. So I can get back to thinking about something besides Jewel Caraway.

But nothing happened during the night. Buck made no move to attack Jewel.

Colin joined the group for breakfast and downed enough coffee to make an elephant jumpy. He thought Buck had wanted to fish for halibut, but the yacht cruised toward a new destination that only Buck knew—a surprise, he'd said.

Doubts suffused Colin's thoughts. If he

was the attacker, the killer, then Buck had successfully stayed two steps ahead of Colin all this time. Jewel was right. Colin couldn't maintain this pace. All he could do was bide his time for Buck to make a mistake or for something else to come through. Something like his memory finally clicking into gear and telling Colin why the other man seemed so familiar. He knew the man from somewhere, and suddenly he'd showed up here and Jewel was attacked, her life threatened. Colin didn't believe in coincidence.

Jewel's attacker had a partner, a woman. As Colin watched Meral chat with Jewel, he couldn't reconcile that fact with what he saw and knew of Jewel's sister. Meral couldn't be the woman who had rammed Jim Humphrey's monster Suburban into Jewel's Durango. So who could the accomplice be?

Stella refilled his coffee mug, poured more orange juice for Meral and Jewel. The cool breeze picked up and the tablecloth fluttered. Jewel's hair whipped across her face.

She tugged it back behind her ear, looking as though she hadn't slept better than Colin, but she kept up a good front for Meral's sake.

Captain Mike chatted with Buck at the rail, while Gary, the deckhand, manned the helm. Colin had seen Captain Mike come and go from Mountain Cove with his chartered cruises, and the certified Coast Guard Master and his crew were not suspects in Colin's mind.

His phone buzzed in his pocket. They must have been passing through limited cell-tower service. He tugged it out to see he had three texts. Two from David, who was just checking on them. The other from his friend and forensic artist, letting Colin know that he would start working on the sketch of Buck. The text had been sent last night.

Colin had asked him to take off fifteen or so years and remove the beard and wrinkles and extra weight, since most people thickened even in the face as they aged. He hadn't met the man while in Alaska, he didn't think, which meant he had to have run into him while in Texas. Taking those extra years off the sketch might trigger Colin's memory.

He jammed his cell back in his pocket, felt his gun under his jacket, though he made no attempt to hide it. Then realized the yacht had stopped. *The Alabaster Sky* anchored in the waters just off where the Bledsoe Glacier terminus met the water.

A loud crack resounded.

Meral jumped up. "Would you look at that?"

They all rushed to the rail.

"That's called calving," Gary told them. Apparently he was not only a deckhand but an ecologist, and could serve as their tour guide when possible. "When ice breaks from the terminus, the end of a glacier, and falls into the water. That's when it's called an iceberg."

They watched in silent awe as ice broke away and fell into the channel water.

After a few minutes, Buck put his hands on Meral's shoulders. "We've got all day to explore the glacier, ice caves and waterfalls. I hope that won't be too uncomfortable for you, Jewel."

"No, of course not. It's a cruise to explore Alaska. I expected as much."

Colin gauged Jewel's reaction to the news. She didn't appear troubled at thoughts of viewing a waterfall so recently after her fall, but he wondered if maybe she was quaking on the inside. She didn't look at him, avoiding making eye contact. Maybe he had his answer.

Was this all part of Buck's plan?

To lure them out into the wilderness and then act? What kind of policeman, what kind of person, was Colin to let him do it? Except Jewel had the right to make her own decisions, and Colin had no evidence to go on. Nothing he could use to accuse Buck and separate Jewel from her sister. All he could do was try to protect her, watch and wait.

He joined Jewel, Meral and Buck in gearing up to hike on the ice, though they'd wait to don crampons, if necessary, when they met with the official tour guide at the US Forest Service's Bledsoe Glacier Visitor Center.

Taking on his own tour guide role again, Gary explained about the region and the glacier before delivering them. Scratching his chin, he eyed them all, his gaze lingering on Jewel. "Glaciers and ice caves are part of the Alaska tour package, but you need to know up front the dangers. Glaciers are moving sheets of ice. They create the ice caves, and the very nature of that creation also makes them unstable. Translated—they're dangerous. Stay alert and follow the safety guidelines."

Gary prepared to take them to shore. Buck and Meral climbed down the short ladder to the skiff. Jewel positioned herself to follow Meral down.

Colin grabbed her arm, stopping her, and pulled her close. "Jewel, are you sure about this? This will be a strenuous activity. You still have stitches. Bruises. And the waterfall. Are you ready to see another one?"

She pressed her hand over his on her arm. "I'll be fine. Really. If I get tired I can stop and rest. Worst case, I'll whine about it and you can escort me back. But I don't want to let Meral down if I don't have to. I know you don't understand."

"How can I? You haven't told me much."

Jewel frowned and started down again, but Colin didn't let go. "Did you bring your Glock?"

"Why would I? I have you to protect me."

Colin released her to go to the boat and followed after her, his own weapon tucked within reach.

They met Preston Jenkins, the professional tour guide, at the center and geared up to hike across the glacier, wearing helmets, backpacks, crampons and carrying ice axes. Colin had lived in southeast Alaska for fifteen years, and he'd never actually hiked a glacier. His experience in this region usually involved getting in and out quickly in a helicopter when there was a need with search and rescue or recovery.

To his way of thinking, hiking a glacier was like walking on a different planet in a faraway galaxy. And he had absolutely no doubt that without Jenkins's skills, they would never have found the ice cave—there was no path that Colin could see.

But after four hours of the most difficult hiking he'd ever experienced, he knew he wouldn't have agreed to this if he'd realized the exertion required. Uneven steps, some places muddy and slippery, scrambling over rock and ice. Meral and Buck's tirelessness surprised him. He was more worried about Jewel with her injuries.

They approached the edge of the glacier on the far side and climbed down to dirt and boulders and pebbles. Jenkins announced that they'd reached the entrance to the cave and allowed them to catch their breaths. The glacier ice was gray and dirty and folded over into the ground, disappearing into an opening, a swirling hole that called them. Finding the cave had been like searching for hidden treasure, and even from the entrance, Colin could see on the inside it shimmered like a gem.

Jenkins led them on, and they followed single file into a whole new world—stunning and strange with cerulean and blue-green ice that had the appearance of glass-like transparent obsidian blooming above them. Colin stood in awe as he stared up at what looked like waves that billowed and rolled—the underside of a river that had been flash frozen.

He couldn't believe he'd lived near such beauty and had never before taken the time to see it. Rocks protruded from patches of ice where they walked. Colin stumbled but caught himself, which pulled his thoughts from the mesmerizing cave of ice and back to the dangers they faced—both from the environment and from the potential killer in their midst. Water trickled and dripped. The cave formed as the glacier melted. For the moment at least, Colin wasn't worried about Buck's intentions—he, too, stumbled around in the cave, head up, neck twisted, humbled by the sight if his reaction was anything like Colin's.

"Looks like chunks are splitting up there, ready to fall down on us. With all this water dripping, I'm going to be soaking wet." Buck hadn't been talking to anyone in particular, then he glanced at Colin. "Kind of creepy, isn't it?"

Colin nodded, but he wasn't thinking about the ice. The way Buck stared at him, grinning; he had a strange feeling the guy knew as much. What was his game? What was he up to?

"How much farther?" Buck called to Jenkins.

"It's a ways. Nothing you can't handle. We can go back at any time."

"What do you think, Meral?"

She glanced at Jewel, who nodded. "I'm

good if you are. I've never seen anything like this. I'm not ready to leave yet."

Jenkins led them deeper into the bowels of the cave. The ice swirled over and around. The group was silent, taking it all in, and Colin admitted it was just a little terrifying. Ice caves had been known to collapse without warning—they were constantly shifting and changing with the glacier, melting off, blocks of ice tumbling.

Despite being enraptured with the natural beauty of their surroundings, Colin never let Jewel out of his sight, albeit peripheral vision at moments. He remained near and stood between her and Buck at all times. Had his weapon ready to use if needed.

Jewel paused to rest on a boulder, and Colin waited with her while the others continued exploring deeper inside the cave.

"How are you doing?" he asked.

Colin was surprised at her agility, especially after her injuries. But she'd spent the past twenty years hiking the wilderness and exploring on a regular basis. He supposed it shouldn't surprise him she would bounce back so easily.

She rubbed her leg while glancing intermittently at Jenkins, Buck and Meral, who had entered another tunnel.

Jenkins hung back. "You guys coming? We need to stay together."

Jewel nodded. "We'll be right there."

He didn't look convinced, but disappeared into the tunnel, his voice echoing with Buck's and Meral's.

"This trip seemed like a good idea," she whispered. "A way for me to be safely away from Mountain Cove, but we're not safe, Colin."

She looked up at him, her hazel eyes looking blustery and taking on the crystal blues of the cave. He thought they'd already agreed on that last night when she'd answered the door holding a Glock.

"When I told you to get away, this wasn't what I meant," he said. "Jewel, I know you want to spend time with Meral, but maybe we should let them continue the cruise without us. You and I will get off right here and now. We'll go back to the visitor center and say our goodbyes." He almost held his breath waiting for her answer, hoping she'd agree.

She hung her head. "It seems ridiculous. We're like two couples on a romantic cruise, but you're my bodyguard. Anyway it doesn't matter. I can't do this anymore. So, yes, let's stop this charade. Me pretending I'm enjoying myself, that I'm not worried about my safety. I don't know about you, but I got next to no sleep last night. I'm sure you didn't either. But...Colin...let me be the one to break it to Meral, okay?"

"Okay." Colin was interested to see how Buck would react. "How are you going to explain it to her?" He'd like to hear that answer from Jewel. He prided himself in his ability to ask the hard questions, but he hadn't yet pushed Jewel for answers the way he should. It was long past time he did. "Why do you believe you're in danger on this venture with your sister and her husband, with me, the police chief, as your bodyguard?"

Footfalls crunched. Jewel watched the tunnel and shook her head. The timing was no good.

Jenkins approached and gave Jewel a concerned look. "We need to get moving. You think you can make it?"

She nodded. "Of course."

He led them down the tunnel to join Buck and Meral and then through a tight space, where they brushed against an ice wall and had to move single file. Colin looked up at the cracks in the ice, the icicles, frozen spears, hanging above. This wasn't safe, but he could almost understand why people risked so much to come here in spite of the dangers. It was a sight one couldn't see anywhere else.

"Meral," Jewel whispered.

Meral slowed and let distance grow between her and Buck.

"Meral, listen, I'm not going to stay on the yacht. I thought I could do this, but I can't."

Buck stopped and turned. "What's that?"

Colin tensed. He would have waited until they were back at the visitor center, had their gear in hand, and could stand on the dock and wave goodbye. He'd assumed she would wait to break the news.

Meral appeared hurt and shocked. She grabbed Jewel's arm.

Colin took a step toward them. Instinct. Reflex to put himself in position to intervene, if necessary.

"What do you mean, Jewel? This trip is for you to keep you safe. To get away. Please, no, you have to stay with us. I'm worried about you."

"Maybe Jewel's injuries are too much for her to enjoy all of this." Buck had joined the conversation now.

Was that all part of his plan? Bring her out here and wear her down? But why? What was he after? This wasn't unfolding the way

Colin would have wanted or expected. Was he even any help at all?

"Is that it, Jewel? Is this too much? I'm sorry for pressuring you," Meral said.

"Well, then, let's make it through the cave and we can just rest on the yacht. We have it for ten days, and in that time we don't have to do any more strenuous activities," Buck said.

He sounded like he was a man who cared, but Colin wasn't fully convinced—and Jewel didn't seem to be either. It was clear to Colin that she didn't trust her brother-in-law. What was less clear was *why*.

Maybe it all went back to what she knew and refused to tell Colin. He'd been a fool not to press her until he got answers. He must be in much deeper than he could admit. The mayor's words about Colin's feelings for Jewel—that she could see it so easily— should have been warning enough that his feelings were impacting his judgment.

He tried to shove his emotions aside, but it was too late. He was already there with Jewel.

Jewel opened her mouth to speak, but Colin cut her off. "That'll work. You guys can do the hard stuff. Jewel and I will just relax on the yacht."

She glanced at him. That wasn't what she'd intended. *Please, just let it be. Read it in my gaze, Jewel.* They could announce their plans to leave the cruise, leave Meral and Buck, once they were back.

"Do you think you can make it through the cave?" Meral asked. "Or should we go back now?"

"Going back or forward makes no difference from this point," Jenkins said. "The distance is about the same since we're going to circle around anyway. Might as well make the most of it instead of backtracking over terrain we've already seen."

Meral and Buck stared at Jewel, waiting for an answer. "Yes, of course, I can make it the rest of the way. I'm sorry I brought it up now. We could have talked about this later."

"Everybody good?" Jenkins tried to hide his scowl and look like a patient tour guide, then marched on.

The ice tunnel opened up into a deep and wide cavern with jagged ice sculptures at the bottom. Jewel and Colin both hung back far from the edge while Meral and Buck boldly moved forward to get the best view. Despite her clear nervousness, Jewel kept inching forward to be close to Meral as though concerned for her. Colin had to maintain his stance between Jewel and Buck just in case the man got any ideas. He wished he had pushed for going back instead of completing the circle.

Jenkins shared his vast knowledge of the ice cave and all things glacier related, and Colin eyed Jewel—so beautiful. He'd often seen that same look of awe on her face. She loved nature. The Alaska wilderness. If he knew anything about her, he knew that. Still, in the midst of her admiration for the beauty around them, she appeared distracted.

Seeing her concern for Meral, Colin ushered her back away from the ledge. "I'll watch out for her," he whispered, and left Jewel resting on a rocky outcropping.

Colin went back to stand next to Meral. Jenkins pointed up at the icicles as one broke off and fell to the bottom, where it shattered like glass. Cut like glass, too. Caught up in the man's voice, Colin looked up at the rest of the glass knives hanging in the cavern.

He felt something at his back. A shove, a push...or a nudge. Reacting, he jerked around.

Then he slipped.

And suddenly the deep cavern loomed ahead. He was falling, sliding on the ice. Desperation and survival skills had him twisting around, reaching for the unforgiving ice, hoping he could stop his fall.

Voices cried out, echoing through the cave. Someone screamed his name.

Heart pounding, he reached for something, anything solid to grab hold of, when a hand grasped his.

Buck held on to Colin, his grip strong and sure. Jenkins dropped prostrate, belly down on the ice, and anchored himself. He grabbed Colin's other hand. "We've got you."

Colin's feet dangled precariously over the cavern, and he couldn't gain any traction against the wall even with crampons. His life depended on these two men.

Pulse racing away and roaring in his ears, Colin stared into Buck's eyes. Familiar eyes. Shadowy, malicious eyes, yet Buck had caught Colin, stopped his fall to certain death. Was even now pulling him back to the ledge. The men heaved and pulled Colin all the way, and they all fell back onto the ledge. Colin crawled away from it completely. Sat with his knees to his chest and tried to catch his breath.

What had just happened?

Jenkins started in on him for slipping to begin with. For getting too close. But that wasn't how it had gone down. He eyed Buck. He thought the man was a killer. Colin had been pushed, enough to cause him to slip, but minor enough so it hadn't been obvious. Who had done it?

Confusion crawled over him. *Had* he been pushed, or had it been his imagination? This must be how Jewel had felt with all the questions. Yet why push him only to save him? Jewel's arms slid over his shoulders and then around him as she plopped onto the iced rocks next to him.

She pressed her face into his shoulder. "That was close, too close."

Who did he think he was, trying to protect her? He hadn't adequately identified the true danger and had nearly died himself. He'd suspected Buck and now the man had saved him.

He watched Buck, who'd taken Meral into

his arms, and the man stared back, his eyes cold and hard and…laughing.

One question ran through Colin's mind.

Who are you really, Buck Cambridge?

TWELVE

Jewel thought they would never make it back to the US Forest Service's Bledsoe Glacier Visitor Center. This had to have been the longest hike of her life. She kept replaying the incident in her mind. She'd been watching Meral, listening to the tour guide, when Colin had slipped on that ledge.

She'd thought her heart would drop right into that cavern with him.

Thank You, God. Thank You for saving him.

Her legs had gone weak and hadn't recovered. But they had made it back to the visitor center and now sat at a small round table. Colin and Buck had left to get them all coffee, everyone avoiding the inevitable conversation they must have.

Colin stood with Buck at the counter of the café. They were talking about something. She would never have known by looking at Colin that he'd almost died. He stood tall and confident. She smiled a little to herself, admiring his broad shoulders. How could Colin seem so strong and durable after nearly losing his life? He was like a heavy-duty truck. He was a force to be reckoned with.

As if sensing she was admiring him, he glanced back at Jewel. Watching, always watching. Except for that one moment when he'd let down his guard. Had that been what caused him to slip? Had he been too busy watching out for her and Meral?

She already knew they couldn't continue like this, and Colin's near miss in the ice cave served to confirm she'd made the right decision to leave the travel "fun." Joining Meral and Buck had seemed like the right thing at the time, her only choice. She'd thought she could handle it. But she'd been wrong.

"Jewel, I don't know what I'm going to do

if you leave the cruise Buck arranged for us." Meral's words pulled Jewel back to the moment. "He's already talking about going back to Baltimore when it's over."

Jewel looked into Meral's beautiful, sad eyes. "I'm not ready to say goodbye yet either. I just know I can't go back to the boat." How much could she share with Meral? What could she say that wouldn't hurt her more?

Even if she wanted to stay, she couldn't ask that of Colin.

Jewel couldn't shake the sense that all their lives were in danger. That Colin's role in her troubles, his decision to appoint himself her bodyguard, had made him a target, not just collateral damage like Jed.

Nausea welled inside. If she were to share her thoughts with a therapist, she would probably be diagnosed with paranoia.

Except it's not paranoia if they really are after you.

"Meral." Jewel watched a group of glacier hikers leave. She should have had this conversation a long time ago, but dreaded it. Had hoped to avoid it. She might not get another chance, since Buck always turned up at the worst moments, as if he somehow knew what Jewel was about to say.

"I'm listening, Jewel. I haven't gone anywhere. Say what you've wanted to say to me. What you've been holding back from me. You can be open and honest with me."

"What do you really know about Buck?"

Meral jerked up her chin as though Jewel had slapped her. Whatever she was expecting Jewel to say, this clearly wasn't it. "Why would you ask that? I know all I need to know, okay? I'm in my thirties, for crying out loud, and don't need anyone's approval. How dare you question my judgment."

Jewel frowned. Despite Meral's soft invitation for Jewel to be open and honest, her reaction was anything but inviting.

"Coming from money you have to be careful, so careful."

"You mean like you were with Silas."

"He wasn't after money. I gave it up for him, remember?"

Meral's eyes glistened with unshed tears. "Why are you doing this, Jewel? I came to see you. Buck found you so we could reconnect. Why are you trying to make me question my happiness? Are you...are you jealous of me because I have someone who loves me? Because I'm married?"

Jewel could hardly stand to hear the hurt in her sister's voice. Her heart palpitated.

This was why she'd wanted to avoid this conversation. She loved her sister. Didn't want to hurt her. Jewel had missed her family and hated to do anything that might jeopardize her newfound connection with her sister. She reached for Meral's hand, but Meral jerked it out of reach.

In her eyes, Jewel could see the deep hurt turning to anger. A defense mechanism. She'd seen the same thing in her father's eyes when she'd refused to give up Silas. It had hurt him badly to realize that she placed Silas above her family. So in return he'd turned his pain into anger and had used it against her, disinheriting her.

But Jewel wouldn't give up. She had to try again. She snatched Meral's hand and gripped hard. And deep concern turned to determination. Even if Meral didn't want to listen to her, Jewel would still speak her mind. It could save Meral's life. "I love you. I don't want it to be like this. Please understand. But I can't stand by and watch without saying this. You could be in danger, Meral. Buck is a dangerous man."

Meral's eyes widened, and she brushed at the tears. Then fury replaced the hurt, and Meral pushed slowly to her feet.

"How dare you." Her tone was a low growl.

"Did you tell him what I took years ago?" Jewel asked.

Meral had to know that she had the diamond. Her family had to have figured out that Jewel had taken it. She'd been so foolish to pretend otherwise.

Jewel saw the truth in Meral's eyes. And she saw denial. Meral didn't want to believe Jewel, but Meral had doubts about Buck—doubts she'd tried to ignore all along. Jewel saw them there as plain as day. She knew her sister. They were flesh and blood, and even after twenty years she knew her.

"There's no need for you to come aboard the yacht for your things." Meral had turned cold. "I'll get them packed up and delivered to you here."

"You're just going to leave us stranded."

"You said you couldn't go back. Now you don't have to. You'll find a ride home, I'm sure. After all, you have the chief of police following you around wanting to be a guard dog, but acting more like a puppy in love."

Jewel stood, too, feeling the ice behind Meral's words and the agony of her own so strongly that her pain was physical. "Meral, I would never do anything to hurt you. I love you. I'm trying to protect you. Please, don't do this. Don't end our time together like this."

"You haven't changed one bit, Jewel. I remember how you were so self-righteous when you left with Silas, not even caring that you were hurting Mom and Dad and me the way you did. Just leaving us all for a man you hardly knew. And don't say I'm doing the same thing. This isn't anything like what you did."

Jewel lowered her voice so she could be sure that only Meral heard her. They had already drawn the men's attention. "You're right. It isn't. You're in love with a murderer who is using you to get what he wants."

The Krizan Diamond. But Jewel was afraid to say it out loud.

Meral flinched. "How do you know this? If Buck was guilty, your man would have already arrested him. But he's not. There's nothing you can prove."

Could it be true? Was Jewel blind to the truth or being paranoid? "Please tell me you're not involved in this." She instantly regretted the words. "I'm sorry, Meral, I didn't mean it. I could never doubt you like that."

But the damage had been done. Icy daggers shot from Meral's eyes. "And yet you doubt my choice of husband. Buck has his own money. He doesn't need mine or yours." Meral stiffened. She glanced across the space to Buck, who held two coffees and was headed their way.

He closed the distance quickly and was at her side, with a curious, mischievous half smile for Jewel.

"Buck, I'm ready to head back to the yacht."

"Yes, my sweet." He kissed Meral's head, but where she couldn't see he had a cruel, mocking expression on his face. Even if he wasn't guilty, he was still a creep.

"We'll pack Colin's and Jewel's things, and the staff can drop them here."

"Are you sure?" Buck set the coffees on the table and turned her to look him in the face. "After all, I went to a lot of trouble to find her and arrange this wedding gift for you.

I'd hate for you to regret this decision later. Once we cross this bridge, I'm not sure we'll be turning back."

"I'm sure. Don't worry. It's not your fault that your gift of a jewel turned out to be a fake."

Acrid. Who could have thought the woman could be so acerbic to her sister?

Colin could hardly stand to watch the scene unfolding before his eyes. On the one hand, he would be glad to see Meral and Buck gone and out of Jewel's life. Maybe that would end the attacks. He just wanted to get Jewel somewhere safe. But on the other hand, seeing her hurting about undid him. And he still believed Buck was responsible for the death of one of his officers. He needed to catch Buck when the man made a mistake. Colin needed evidence to make his arrest.

He'd heard the mayor loud and clear.

If he was going to come back, he needed to return with the bad guy. He was on the case of his life and career. It all surrounded a woman he cared deeply about. And he couldn't seem to see a way to get Jewel to safety while still catching the criminal.

As Buck ushered Meral out of the visitor center, Jewel pressed her face into her hands, her shoulders shaking. That had been one very public scene. Colin moved next to her and sat down. He held his hand above her back, her shoulder, hesitating, wanting to comfort her, but fearing his growing emotional attachment to this woman.

This is about her. Not you.

Colin pressed his hand on her shoulder and squeezed. He leaned in close to whisper. But what could he say to her when she was hurting like this?

His heart pricked. Anger tangled up with feelings so deep he couldn't fathom them. He wanted to run after Meral and stop her from going away like this, but he knew there was nothing he could say. If Meral wouldn't listen to Jewel, then she certainly wouldn't listen to him.

"Jewel," he said gently in her ear. People were still staring. He had to get her somewhere private.

This was a woman who had left behind family and wealth to move to a harsh land for the man she loved, and then had learned to run her business on the edge of the wilderness on her own after her husband was gone. Jewel could have gone back home, but she'd chosen to stay. She'd been so strong for so very long.

And now she appeared broken.

Reconnecting with her family had ended in heartache, after all.

Jewel sat up straight and wiped her eyes. Drew in a breath and looked at him. Though the grief he saw there was a punch in his gut, he recognized her determination had returned.

Attagirl.

She stood then and waited for him to join her.

"I have to go back to the yacht."

"What? After all that, you want to go back? You can't be serious."

"Dead serious."

Time for Colin to stop coddling. Time for him to make his own demands. "No."

She stood and attempted to walk by him. He grabbed her arm and swung her around, keeping his grip gentle but implacable, ushering her toward the restaurant at the back. Leaning in as they walked, he spoke in her ear. "Listen to me." He kept his voice low. "You can't go back to the boat."

"You can't stop me."

Finding a booth in the corner, Colin practically forced her in.

"You know I can use those self-defense techniques you taught me on you, right?" she said.

Colin slid in next to her, blocking her exit. "Then why didn't you?"

"Why are you doing this?" Her eyes pleaded. "I have to go before they leave."

Colin needed to keep her here long enough

to miss the boat, but her pleas tugged at his heart. "This is life-and-death, Jewel."

Something he couldn't read flashed in her eyes, and she backed against the wall.

"What do you mean?"

"I think you know what I mean." Time to ask those hard questions and get answers. "Your sister's husband is a dangerous man. And I think you know that, too."

THIRTEEN

Trapped.

She was jammed against the wall in the booth. The yacht would leave without her unless she headed to the dock soon. But Colin clearly wouldn't let her go until he'd gotten some answers, and he was right. So right. Right that Buck was dangerous, right that she knew it and right that it was a matter of life-and-death. She shouldn't go back, except she'd left something there. How did she make him understand?

His actions should incense her, but deep down she recognized how much he cared about her. His nearness and her predicament had her heart beating erratically. She'd done well to try to protect it, but the recent threats on her life made her vulnerable. She was too busy trying to stay alive and trying to keep Meral safe, too, and she'd let down her guard.

Protectiveness poured off this man, who had her cornered, and his stark blue eyes took her in as though trying to soak her up. A warm shiver ran over her. Jewel had never thought she could love someone like she had loved Silas. And maybe she couldn't. She was a different person now than she'd been twenty years ago, and that giddy love-conquers-all optimism had worn away. But could she be ready for a new kind of love?

With Colin's sturdy form blocking her way—protecting her—maybe it was more that she was afraid to love again. She had a feeling that Colin could be that man if only she'd let him in.

But she shoved those thoughts away. She had to get to *The Alabaster Sky.*

"You're right. He is dangerous. That's exactly why I have to go back."

"To save Meral? You think she'll listen?" Colin's tone challenged.

No. She'd tried to stop Meral. Make her see the light about Buck, but her sister wanted too badly to believe that she'd found her happily-ever-after. She wouldn't listen to a word against Buck. And anyway, there was more to her need to return to the boat than that. More that Colin didn't know. "You don't understand."

She slid toward Colin, acting as though she expected him to move out of her way. But he didn't budge, and now she sat closer to him.

"Then make me understand, Jewel. Tell me what you haven't been willing to tell me before now. I'm done skirting the real issue, dancing around it."

She hadn't wanted to tell him the whole truth at first because she couldn't bear to see his disappointment in her. And then she had hung on to the slim hope she was wrong about Buck. But now? Colin needed to know it all because she'd been wrong to withhold it. She saw that now.

And telling him, seeing his reaction to the truth, would go a long way in burying anything she might otherwise have with him. She drew in a breath, fortified herself.

"Have you ever done something that completely went against everything you are or believed in? Something that you've regretted for the rest of your life?"

"Yes, Jewel. I think we've all done that."

"Years ago, I took something valuable that didn't belong to me, and I left it on the boat."

He paled. "Something worth killing for?"

"I believe so, yes."

"Why didn't you tell me about this before?"

"It doesn't matter. I have to get it back."

"Tell me what it is and where you've hidden it, and I'll get it for you."

"There are things you don't know about me, Colin. For starters, I come from an old-money, wealthy family back east."

The words didn't seem to faze him. Did he

already know? But he couldn't know the rest, and she had to tell him quickly. They were running out of time. "I was in my early twenties when I went on a cruise in Alaska with some friends and I met Silas. That weekend, as he showed us the wilderness and nature, I fell in love with this place. But it didn't end there. Silas and I…we had a connection. It seemed crazy. I thought I'd never see him again, but he followed me home and even though it sounds old-fashioned, he courted me. At the time, my family thought he was after our money."

Jewel shifted. Dragged in air. She was doing this. Really doing this. "They did everything they could to keep us apart, but I was in love and wouldn't listen. Silas made me feel alive. And I knew he didn't care about the money, so I planned to elope with him. My father got wind of it and threatened to disinherit me if I went through with it. I knew he was serious—that once I left with Silas, he wouldn't accept me back into the family, even if I came back a few months later and said it had all been a mistake. Risking everything like that for Silas…it scared me. I guess that I wasn't completely convinced it wasn't all a dream. I figured if the worst happened, then I wanted something to fall back on, some security. I didn't have my own money, not in any significant way, and now I see that was a way they controlled me. But there was something else I could get to—something valuable."

Colin leaned closer, intent on her story. "What did you take?"

"I took the Krizan Diamond. It's a family heirloom from an ancient mine in India. It was handed down to my mother, whose family founded Simmons Diamonds. My father married into the business. They groomed me to be part of that business, too. But diamonds are cold and hard and lifeless and don't give love, so I left it all behind for Silas. Except for…the Krizan Diamond. It's worth a small fortune."

He paled and slid away from her in the booth. His move was subtle, but she'd seen it.

It was just as she'd feared. He thought less of her now for stealing a diamond and harboring it in her home—not to mention keeping the information from him. She didn't blame him. But what would he, an officer of the law, do with her now? She wasn't a jewel thief in the typical sense. And once this was over, though she couldn't see how it would end, she was willing to give the diamond back to her family, to Meral. Jewel no longer needed it. No longer wanted it.

In fact, she had never needed it. But she'd been afraid to trust completely.

With Colin's reaction, she saw that perhaps she had been wrong to trust him with the truth.

"Why did you bring the diamond?"

"All these years I had it hidden away in the attic, but with the attacks I suspected that someone might be after it. I've suspected Buck all along. Learning that a woman had driven the truck that rammed me made me doubt my suspicions because I just couldn't believe that Meral would be involved. I thought to put it in a safe-deposit box, but I couldn't get away. And then if I brought it with me on the boat and the attacks continued or the diamond was stolen, I would know for sure that Buck had been behind the attacks."

Maybe. Saying it out loud now, she wasn't sure it made any sense.

"And you didn't trust me enough to tell me?"

"Telling you about it meant implicating Buck. I didn't want to believe it could be him. I wasn't sure. But now I have to go."

"No, Jewel. I can't let you go. Buck won't get away. Don't worry. Now I need you to stay here."

"Where are you going?"

Something shifted behind Colin's gaze. It was cold, hard. Professional. "Now that you've told me the truth, I know what I'm dealing with and I need to make a phone call. Promise me you will wait here until I get back."

Jewel didn't want to give him that promise.

"I'm telling you this as an officer of the law, Jewel."

"Am I…am I under arrest?"

He frowned. "Get serious."

Right. The statute of limitations had expired. But she'd kept pertinent information to herself that could have helped him solve this case. Still, what she'd told him had disturbed him far deeper than she would have expected.

She saw that clearly in his eyes. He'd pulled away from her physically. And emotionally. Though she'd protected her heart from falling for this man, the intense pain shooting through her chest illuminated that she was more than halfway there.

Colin stumbled from the booth. Could he trust Jewel to stay? He had no choice. He needed a moment to regain his composure.

His vision tunneled as his past swirled before him.

A jewel thief.

I know where I've seen Buck before.

Brock Ammerman.

Buck Cambridge.

Buck Cambridge *was* Brock Ammerman, the jewel thief who had murdered Katelyn twenty years ago. But he was dead. Colin had killed him.

He staggered. Pressed his hand against the wall for support.

It can't be. How can it be?

His cell buzzed. What now? He pulled it from his pocket absently, going through the motions by rote. He must be losing his mind. He didn't believe in coincidences, but neither did he believe in the impossible.

Colin glanced back at Jewel to make sure she was waiting. Her gaze shifted around the room as if she were looking for an exit, but he was blocking the only one.

The text was from the forensic artist. He'd

sent the picture he'd created after taking off the years—Brock Ammerman.

Buck Cambridge *is* Brock Ammerman. The man had changed so much over twenty years, and Colin had thought him dead anyway. Little wonder he hadn't been able to place him.

Colin leaned completely against the wall.

Not possible.

How? How could this be? He'd killed this man in self-defense. The charges against Ammerman hadn't stuck, and Colin had wanted to kill him. He had wanted to exact revenge, but that hadn't been his motivation when he'd followed Brock that day. He'd just wanted to warn him that he would put him behind bars for good one day—let him know that it wasn't over. Then when Brock had tried to kill him in response, knowing that Colin would always be watching, Colin had gotten the upper hand and killed the man in self-defense. One bullet to the chest had taken him out for good.

But it had all looked suspicious, and Colin had been put on leave while the department had investigated. It hadn't helped that Katelyn's family had wanted him to pay for her death. Had that all been part of Brock's plan?

But how Brock had survived, he still didn't know. Had someone working within the department helped Brock fake his own death? Had it all been big conspiracy?

No. Colin wouldn't believe that for a minute. His cell buzzed. *Not now. Not now.* He didn't have time. He glanced at it. David Warren. If he didn't answer, David might send the Coast Guard looking.

"Yeah, David," Colin said. "I can't talk for long. I'm…in the middle of something."

"You okay? Cuz you don't sound okay."

"It's too much to explain right now, but I think it's all coming to a head. And I have to figure it out."

Colin had to pull himself together. He still didn't have enough evidence to make an arrest for murder. His story was a tangled mess, as was Jewel's. It would take more than a phone call to untangle it, and Buck still wouldn't be arrested for Jed's murder and the attacks on Jewel. He might disappear altogether.

But one thing Colin knew. Brock was dead. He'd killed the man himself, so what was going on?

Lord, help me to see the truth here.

"Maybe I can help." A giggle resounded over the phone that didn't belong to David.

"Where are you?" Colin asked.

"I'm off today. Tracy's working at the B and B. I can't wait until this is over so I can get my wife back. I never see her. Right now I've got the boys."

Colin nodded absently, thinking of David and Tracy's twin sons.

"So what's up? Tell me what's going on. Do I need to come and get you and Jewel?"

Twins.

"No, not yet. I've got to go now, but just know this, David, your phone call helped."

He made a quick call to his friend back in

Texas to start looking for answers. Did Brock Ammerman have a twin?

Colin paced, calming his heart rate so he could function.

Jewel was sitting back there waiting for him to return. What would he tell her? Think. He had to think.

Why would Buck come all the way to Alaska for the diamond? His wife had access to wealth and jewels via her family. Except…if they were willing to disinherit their oldest daughter for marrying without their approval, then he doubted they would allow Buck into the circle, giving him access to anything of value. But maybe it was more than that. Brock's targets hadn't been high profile. Meral and Jewel's family would definitely be a high-profile family, the theft creating too much noise, and the jewels couldn't be fenced so easily or quickly.

That had to be it.

Buck had convinced Meral to come to Alaska because he'd found out about Jewel's secret. Add that Colin was here as chief of police, and Buck must have seen it as a way to get the prize and revenge all at once. Maybe that was why he killed Jed. To get back at Colin for Brock's death. But he might not be finished with his killing spree.

Colin blew out a breath to erase those morbid images that had sent him running to Alaska to start afresh. Brock had murdered Katelyn—and now Brock, or rather his twin, was here close to…Jewel.

And poor Jewel, carrying the weight of believing she'd stolen the diamond, when he could easily see a loving mother making sure her young daughter had taken something of value by either planting the seed or allowing her access. But what did he know about it? That was all conjecture.

Everything he had right now was conjecture. He needed the facts. No matter how much he listened to his gut, his instincts wouldn't hold up in a court of law. He'd been right to follow his gut this far, sure, but he needed to seal the deal. Find the evidence behind the attacks on Jewel. But he could figure that out. Right now he had to get back to her. He turned to enter the restaurant again.

Jewel was gone.

FOURTEEN

"Your sister's husband is a dangerous man."
She should have waited on him. He'd made
it clear when he'd pulled the police card. The
chief-of-police card, rather. But she'd also
gotten that he wasn't going to let her go back
to the yacht, where she needed to be. As soon
as his focus had turned from her, she'd fled
the booth.

Hearing Colin say that Buck was a dangerous man had infused her with determination.
She couldn't let Meral leave with that man,
even though he was her husband. But how to
get her away? How did Jewel convince her?

After slipping through the window in the
restroom, she dropped to the ground. Hemlock, spruce and cedar hid her from view.

She'd never done anything like this before. Well, other than taking the diamond. But she had to get to the yacht. She had to save Meral, if she could, and retrieve the diamond while she was at it.

Buck wasn't going to hurt Jewel in broad daylight in front of the crew or Meral. She could try one more time to save her sister, despite Meral's vitriolic words.

Pressing her back against the log wall of the visitor center, she hoped Colin hadn't discovered her gone yet, but he would soon enough. She had to hurry.

She'd seen him on the phone. Had he been checking on old warrants for her arrest for stealing a diamond? The statute of limitations was only a few years, but that wouldn't make her any less a thief to him. She'd seen the shock in his eyes turn to pure disappointment.

Her words had shaken him as much as his reaction had crushed her. But she was a woman who was destined to lose at love.

She was glad she hadn't actually been playing that game with Colin. Only toying with the idea.

More importantly, she had to protect her sister and survive another encounter with the man after her life.

No more time to think about Chief Colin Winters, and, yes, she should think of him in official terms from now on. He'd made that much clear.

She crept to the corner of the building and peeked around. In the distance the yacht was still anchored in the channel. Had Meral and Buck been taken back yet? If she hurried, she could make it before they left.

Jewel sagged against the wall. A cedar branch tickled her arm. Part of her wanted to give up. It would be easier to sink to the ground and cry for all she had lost—a list that now included her sister for a second time.

Meral's life could be in serious danger. She could disappear on the cruise. Be pushed overboard, and Buck would likely gain her money, holdings and benefit from an insurance policy as well as obtain the Krizan Diamond either by finding and stealing it or by killing Jewel.

What am I supposed to do now, God? None of this makes any sense.

Why did You let this happen to me? I was doing okay at the B and B. I had made a life of my own already. I didn't need the past to come roaring back.

"As far as the east is from the west, so far has he removed our transgressions from us." Psalm 103:12

Don't You shove the past, our sins, as far as the east is from the west? I even have one of those cross-stitches Katy makes in one of the rooms. Maybe You did remove my transgression, but I've kept my sin close, hidden in the attic and buried away until now. And I'm sorry for that. So sorry.

Jewel shook off the weight of guilt. She could worry about that later.

A pain pierced her side. The muzzle of a

gun. Jewel stiffened and gasped. She turned, but a grip forced her to keeping staring ahead. In the distance, *The Alabaster Sky* began heading out into the channel.

"Looks like your past has caught up to you." The familiar voice whispered in her ear.

"What's going on? Why is the yacht leaving without you? Where is Meral?" *God, please don't let Meral be involved. Please keep her safe.*

"Your sister is safe and sound on the yacht. She won't even know I'm gone."

"Are you saying that you drugged her?"

"Works like a charm. She never even realizes that she's missing time. She doesn't have a clue that you hold her life in your hands."

Jewel gasped.

Colin, come on. Find me. Notice I'm gone!

She'd wanted to escape before Colin found her, and now she wished he would hurry up. He hadn't let her out of his sight until now. Was he still freaking out over what she'd told him? Still on his phone?

"Come on." Buck pushed her away from the visitor center and through the trees, away from the center's entrance and the channel where *The Alabaster Sky* had been anchored.

Jewel thought to fight him. She wouldn't go willingly. She tensed, preparing to use a self-defense move, but he pressed the weapon to the base of her skull. Fear corded her neck. Could she fight him and live?

"Don't even think about it. Remember, you have to think of Meral. You fight me and I'll make sure she suffers before I kill her."

"What kind of monster would kill his own wife?" But she knew. She knew what kind of monster. He was a con artist. He'd never loved Meral. Jewel had seen that from the beginning.

Buck had turned desperate and was showing his true self now. What had happened to change his tactics?

He grabbed her hair, sending shards of pain through her head, and shoved her deeper into the woods. Then suddenly he stiffened. He yanked her close and stepped behind a broad cedar tree. Pulling her against his body, he wrapped his free arm around her waist and thrust the gun against the side of her head.

He pressed his lips against her ear and whispered, making her shudder. "One word and you're dead. Think of Meral."

He was pure evil in human form. She squeezed her eyes shut, trying to stop the tears. She'd known, felt it all along.

What had he heard? Someone following?

Was it Colin?

Please, God!

A minute, maybe two he waited, and with his proximity those seconds felt like an eternity. She was so close she instantly felt when the tension drained from him. His fear of discovery had gone.

He whispered again. "I'm warning you, Jewel, don't try your lame self-defense tactics on me. A firearm is the great equalizer. Even if you were a match for me, I'm the one with the gun. I've been impressed with your resilience; I'll give you that. The way you survived that tumble into Dead Man Falls. That alone should have killed you."

He grabbed her hair and shoved her forward and away from the tree.

Jewel stumbled over a root and fell. He didn't relinquish his hold on her hair, so she cried out, the pain searing. She was sure he would rip her hair out of her scalp. Her eye burned.

"Get up," he snapped.

Using her hands to grab his on her head, she stood up, or more likely she was pulled to her feet. She wanted to do her part to make the slow going even slower, to stall as much as she could. Maybe someone would see them. Maybe Colin would finally discover she was gone and catch up to them. But if she delayed his plans, then the monster would do much worse than rip out her hair before it was over. Kill her and then Meral.

They marched deeper through the undergrowth that ended when it banked against the glacier.

"Why kill me? Why not just take what you want?"

Where was he taking her? Why back toward the glacier?

"Because I couldn't get to it—or thought I couldn't. Our second day at your B and B, I heard you mention to Meral that you'd willed everything to her years ago after your husband died, your way to connect back to your family. Your death would have meant Meral had access to the diamond. I figured you had it in a safe-deposit box in a bank like most people. One quick shove into Dead Man Falls and it would be mine. But no, you had to survive that. Good thing, too. When I saw you sneak up to the attic I knew why."

"How? How could you know?" She turned to face him.

"The same way I know you brought the diamond with you on this trip. I've made a living reading people who have things to hide." He smacked her across the face. Her eyes watered again. "That's for making me work so hard for it."

Cheek burning, Jewel pressed her palm against her face.

"Keep going."

She stood her ground. "Where are we going? Why don't you just ask me what you want to know? Why drag me out here?"

"All in good time. We have to get away from your knight in shining armor first. He's probably on his way to the yacht to look for you. Good thing I made it more difficult. I underestimated you, Jewel. You know how to hide things. Now I've had to go to extreme measures. Things would have been so much easier if you had just died any of the times when you were supposed to."

He pressed her forward. Jewel shivered, growing tired. Through the forested incline she could see the icy edges of the glacier only a few yards down where it hedged against the mountain on its journey to the channel. Jewel stumbled and fell to her knees again, but this time Buck did not have a hold on her hair.

He grabbed her arm and jerked her up. Jewel cringed from the pain. He ushered her forward and down, then around a crack in the ice and shoved her into an opening—a cold chute into another ice cave, different from the one they'd explored earlier.

"Why are you taking me here?" How did he know about this cave at all?

He forced her ahead of him into the cave without crampons or backpack or gear. Her gloves were stashed in her pack. At least she still wore her jacket. As she climbed over icy boulders and slipped a few times, she was positive this was off the tourist path. Then he shoved her to the ground, where she fell between two boulders and cut her hand on the ice.

"Nobody will find you here."

"So you mean to succeed in killing me this time."

"It's simple, really. If you tell me where

the diamond is, you can go back to your police chief and sister. I'll disappear. When she wakes up, you get to tell her I'm gone. Tell her the truth about why or not. It's up to you. But either way I'll disappear with the diamond."

Jewel didn't believe him. Why would he let her go? She could then be a witness against him if he was ever caught. No, once she told him where to find it, he would kill her.

Jewel pushed up to sitting, the best she could. Pain jabbed her from new injuries and echoed from her recent ones—all due to Buck's attacks. If only she could have confronted him from the beginning.

"You can't just sell a diamond like that. It won't work."

He laughed. A strange sound coming from him.

"I'm in the business of imports and exports. What do you think that means? I'm a jewel thief and a fence. I already have the connections. I already have a buyer. All I need is the diamond."

Jewel squeezed her eyes shut. She never could have imagined this twenty years ago when she'd taken what she'd thought would be a safety net.

"Come on, Jewel. The diamond for Meral's life."

"She's your wife."

"And your sister."

"Answer me this, did you ever really love her?"

"She's a beautiful woman with top-notch society connections. Marrying her had more than a few benefits. But what you're missing here is that Meral married *me* for *my* money. She doesn't really love me, although she's convinced herself that she does. She likes to think of it all as a fairy tale. But the truth is she loves that I can provide a comfortable life for her. Her last husband depleted her funds. Meral was broke."

"But if you have money, why go to such

lengths for this diamond? Why marry a woman you don't even love?"

His smirk speared through her. "I'm in business. I must keep generating revenue, and we've had a few hard years."

Jewel hung her head, wanting to get as much truth out of him as she could, if she could trust anything he said. "Does she… Does Meral know the truth about you? Was Meral in on your plans to steal the diamond?"

"No. Meral's habit of turning a blind eye, and not wanting to see the ugly truth of how things really are, is how her first husband got away with draining their accounts. She learned years ago, probably while she was still at home with your family, not to let herself notice things that might upset her and simply look the other way when it suited her. And because she did, you were able to get away with the Krizan Diamond when you stole it and left to marry a poor man. She shared the truth about you and the Krizan Diamond with me, her soul mate, the first night we were together as lovers. That same night I knew I should propose. It's a gift, really. A sixth sense for a big opportunity that has paid off well in business dealings. And Meral accepted. After all, I was charming and had money. Marrying me would benefit her. She dressed it up in more romantic thoughts, but getting married was a mutually beneficial business arrangement."

Jewel nodded, understanding things better now. It fit with the image she had of her sister to learn that Meral wouldn't choose to do something she felt was wrong…but she'd be easily convinced to look the other way when someone else did something wrong—as had Jewel years ago.

"Now time's up," he said. He tugged some plastic straps from his pocket.

"Buck, no. You can't leave me in here, tied up so I can't even move. I'll freeze to death."

He gestured with his head. "You've got your coat. But I stashed a few blankets. You'll be fine. I just need time to verify you've told me the truth. If I find it, then I'll make a call and let someone know where you are. And if I don't, then I'll be back with a piece of Meral."

Right. If he found it, then he would leave her here to die, or come back and kill her himself. Either way she was dead.

Buck shifted toward her, lifted her chin with the muzzle of his gun. "Now, Jewel. Where did you hide the diamond?"

Colin stood outside the cave listening, getting most of what Buck said, but missing a few words.

He'd come around the building in time to see movement in the woods and had followed his gut. Even though *The Alabaster Sky* was already cruising away from the glacier, and Jewel should have been heading that direction trying to catch the boat before it was out of sight, he had listened to his instincts.

That had paid off.

He hadn't gotten a chance to attack Buck,

to free Jewel from his grasp, because the man had had a weapon pointing at her head the whole time. With the trees and brush hindering his view, getting a shot off at Buck would have been too risky.

No. Colin had to wait for the right time, and now that time had come. Buck would be leaving Jewel here. Colin could wait until he left to free her, but if she didn't tell Buck the truth about the diamond, he might kill Meral before he came back for Jewel. There could be another murder on Buck's hands. On Colin's conscience.

Better to arrest the man now after both Colin and Jewel had heard the man's confession. Buck had been the attacker that day at the falls. But he hadn't said a thing about Jed. Colin needed that confession, too. He needed something concrete.

"Winters," the man called from inside the cave. "Come on in."

Heart jumping up his throat, Colin sank away behind the tree. No, no, this wasn't how it was supposed to go down. He'd put in a call for help, but it would take too long for backup to arrive.

"Jewel is waiting for you, Chief Winters. Join the party."

Jewel cried out in pain.

He couldn't leave her in there alone with this murderer. He had no choice and felt as if once again he was becoming entangled in a fight he wasn't smart enough or strong enough to win. If he'd been the first to attack, the one to surprise Buck, then this would all be over.

He hadn't brought his department-issued Glock on this venture, but his personal SIG P224. A compact 9-millimeter pistol he could hide out of sight—which he did, tucking it away carefully under his jacket along with an extra magazine loaded with ammo before he strode into the cave.

Buck pointed his weapon point-blank at Jewel, who sat on the ground. When she glanced up at Colin, sorrow spilled from her gaze, followed by fear and something more.

Determination.

Good girl.

She was doing better than Colin right now. Seeing her helpless, a man aiming a gun on her, nearly drove Colin to his knees. But he kept standing and allowed adrenaline to course through him. Fire up his nerves. Reinforce his muscles.

"Good," Buck said. "I wouldn't expect any less of you. Now, hand over your weapon. The nine millimeter you like to stash out of sight when you're off duty."

A few choice words ran through Colin's head. A few scenarios tortured him. Like pulling out the weapon and firing at Buck. Dropping him then and there. But Jewel. What about Jewel? She could get caught in the cross fire.

He pulled the SIG from his back and set it on the ground. His gaze fell on Jewel, who stared at the ground now. Did she think Colin had failed her? He hadn't given up yet, and if he knew anything about Jewel, she hadn't either. They would get their chance.

"Now kick it over to me and back away." Odd that the man would smile now. "You know, I think I was subconsciously hoping you'd find me here with Jewel. Sure, it would be simpler if this game ends with me getting the diamond and disappearing with no muss and no fuss. But seeing you here makes me happy. You are part of what made it more fun."

"You're demented."

"Oh, you have no idea." He inched away from Jewel, still aiming his weapon at her. Knowing that she was his leverage now.

This was exactly what Colin had hoped to avoid. In the meantime, he needed to keep him talking. Get him talking about himself, buy some time and maybe Colin would get his chance to end this for good.

"You're wondering what I'm still doing alive, aren't you?"

"No. I figured it out. You're Brock's twin brother."

"Took you long enough. You know what

you haven't figured out? Brock wasn't the one to steal those jewels or kill anyone—not the woman getting robbed or your witness, the woman you loved."

Anger boiled, frothing red-hot magma ready to erupt as he thought back to that time.

Colin had been a detective in Texas investigating a jewel thief and murderer. The victim arrived home and surprised the thief. Colin had a witness—the woman's neighbor, Katelyn Morrison. Over time as Colin investigated, even though it was against the rules, Katelyn had become the love of his life. He'd hoped she would say yes when he proposed, but he'd always feared he wasn't good enough—her being independently wealthy while he was just a lowly police officer.

Colin had been near wrapping up the case so he and Katelyn could get on with their lives when she had been murdered. The only witness, the only real evidence, gone. No one had known about his relationship with Katelyn, and he went on to investigate her murder, too. Brock Ammerman had been charged and put on trial. The DNA evidence found at the scene pointed to Brock. But he'd had a solid alibi. He'd been emceeing at a conference two hundred miles away during the time the murder had been committed. Hundreds of witnesses proved that. The DNA evidence at the scene of the crime had been shot down as being tampered with in some way.

Colin hadn't seen that coming. He should have bided his time and gathered more evidence. Buck had gotten away with murdering the woman he loved because Colin had acted too quickly, before all the facts were in and he'd had the wrong man all along—Buck's twin brother, Brock.

Keep talking, Buck, and I just might rush you and kill you with my bare hands.

"That was all me. That's why you couldn't get the conviction. Couldn't make your charges stick, Chief. And it was that kind of planning, because we share the same DNA,

that made Brock and I a successful duo. Part-
ners in crime."

"How did you keep it a secret? How did
others not know you had a twin?"

"Simple. We had no idea either until we
were in our late twenties. We had been
adopted out, separated at birth. I don't think
that's even legal these days. Have you ever
read those stories about twins that are separated? How they dress the same, marry
women with the same name, maybe even pick
the same names for their children?"

Colin nodded, grasping the truth. "You ran
into each other in the same career."

"Trying to steal the same gem. Imagine
our surprise, but we were smart enough to
realize we could use that to our advantage.
Together we were able to exponentially in-
crease our potential as jewel thieves. After
that we wondered how we had ever worked
alone before. And we excelled until you came
along and killed my brother. But you killed
the wrong brother."

"It was in self-defense." Colin wouldn't beg for his life, though.

"You ruined everything. When I learned of the missing diamond from Meral, I did my research and found Jewel easily enough. Giving the gift of a reunion with her sister seemed the fitting thing to do for a wedding present. But I always research the law entities where I'll be working, too, and that's when I discovered you were chief of police in Mountain Cove."

His smile twisted into the familiar smirk. "What a thrill to go another round with you, especially when you had no idea I even existed. I could get my revenge. A life for a life. I could kill the woman you loved. Again. After all, you killed my twin brother."

That was it.

Colin exploded in fury and rammed into Buck.

Gunfire blasted in his ear.

FIFTEEN

Covering her head, Jewel turned and scrambled behind one of the boulders near where she'd been sitting. From there she peered out and prayed for Colin. Bullets ricocheted off the ice walls from two weapons. Colin had grabbed his own gun, and the two fought each other in a deadly battle.

A massive block of ice crashed down, shattering in an explosive display. Fragments hit dangerously close to where Colin wrestled with Buck for the upper hand.

A truck-sized chunk of ice slid across the ground like a bull charging toward her. Jewel pressed against the frozen wall—deeper, harder—turned her face away. Cold seeped through her bones. Sharp edges pinched into her skin. She squeezed her eyes shut. There was nowhere else to go.

She waited for the impact, though it all happened in a millisecond. The deadly ice slammed against the boulder and broke into smaller pieces that slid to a stop near her feet.

Releasing her pent-up breath, she prayed harder. Cried out to God.

If the gun continued firing and more bullets ricocheted, the whole cave might come crashing down on them.

I'm helpless here.

She was no use to Colin.

God, what can I do? Help us, please!

Jewel searched for a rock. But wait. She could use the chunk of ice next to her foot with its sharp, cutting edges.

Maybe.

Carefully gripping the frozen weapon, she crawled from behind the protective boulder. Both men continued their struggle over just one gun now, and it flailed in all directions. Another shot rang out as a bullet whizzed past her ear. Jewel ducked behind the boulder again.

She would be deaf before this was over, if she even survived. If the ice above them didn't react to the concussive blasts, crack and cave in.

What do I do? What do I do?

What if Colin lost this battle? Then what?

Jewel couldn't let that happen. She picked up the broken ice again, as solid as a rock and just as deadly, and charged out into the open. Colin had Buck against the wall, beating his arm and wrist against jagged ice so he would release his weapon.

Buck cried out, fired the weapon, then released it.

Jewel dropped the rock to pick up the gun instead.

But Buck elbowed Colin in the nose and broke loose before grabbing Jewel from behind. Swinging her around to face Colin, Buck had pulled a knife from his pocket and pressed it to her throat. She gripped the gun and tossed it to Colin. It fell to the ground and slid toward him.

In her ear, Buck laughed. "Both guns are out of ammo now, so the gun is no use to the chief."

Had they fired that many rounds? They were fortunate the ceiling hadn't fallen down on them. With her thoughts, a resounding crack split the air. They stood frozen, waiting to see if the ice cave would collapse on them. Even Buck tensed. But nothing happened.

Then she saw it. Colin had been shot. Blood oozed from his shoulder and his nose. He staggered, almost imperceptibly, but she caught it.

Jewel searched Colin's gaze. She wanted to fight back like Colin had taught her. She positioned her feet in a wide stance. But to her surprise, he sent her a subtle shake of his head.

No.

What? He didn't even want her to try?

"Come on." Buck tugged her back and away from Colin.

She held her ground, refusing to move. "You're not going to kill me. Without me, you'll never find the diamond."

"Don't test your theory." He pressed the cold blade harder against her neck. A sharp sting pricked her skin; warmth slid down. Her legs went weak. "And I wouldn't worry about the chief saving you. He's in no shape to follow."

"No!" she screamed as Buck dragged her away, pressing the knife into her throat. "You can't leave him to die."

"Believe me. This is not how I wanted this to end. I wanted him to suffer more."

He dragged her deeper into the ice cave, where the greens and cerulean blues turned dark and ominous. And the deeper they went, the farther she was from Colin. Would he survive? Would she ever see him again? Why hadn't he run after Buck again? He must be badly wounded, possibly dying; otherwise he would come for her.

She twisted, but any movement she made other than forward with Buck meant potential death as she felt the sting of the knife, the small trickle of blood already running down her neck.

"Colin!" she called back to him. Jewel sucked in too much air and won herself another cut. "Listen," she said to Buck. "I'll tell you where the diamond is and you can just let me go. Colin needs help. I can't let him die."

"Why not? He failed you, just like he failed the woman he loved in Texas. Why would you want to help him now? He deserves what he gets."

"You're a monster."

"So I've heard."

"It makes me shudder to think you're married to my sister." She tried to jerk away. "Where are you taking me?"

"Plans have changed. I can't be sure others won't show up looking for the chief or for you, so you'll need to come with me. You can show me the diamond yourself. I might like that better. You can put the diamond in my hand and beg for your life. Let's face it, if I kill you, Meral might inherit everything, but that doesn't mean we'll ever find it. You've hidden it well so far. And my business is overextended at the moment. Taking the diamond from you is like a moonlighting weekend, nothing more."

"Then you should pull the knife away because you're going to accidentally kill me before you have the diamond."

Buck responded. Jewel was free from the knife.

Now that it no longer threatened her within an inch of her life, she pressed her face into her hands, stumbling as she went, thinking of all her regrets.

She'd never really trusted Silas, the man she'd loved, with her life. If she had, she wouldn't have stolen the diamond in the first place, and all of this trouble could have been avoided.

If I had known what the future held, God, I never would have done it! But, God, I want to move past my mistakes. I want to live to see another day. I want a chance at love again.

She wanted a chance to love Colin. What an idiot she'd been not to see that. Not to take a chance at having a complete life again. At loving again.

Maybe…maybe she had loved him all along, but from a distance.

Had she ruined their chance to be together? For all she knew, he could be dying right now. But, no, that wasn't true. Jewel had a feeling, a very strong feeling, that Colin was alive. Or maybe she just refused to believe he would die when he had so much to live for. Together they had so much to live for. And Colin wasn't the sort of man to give up as long as he had breath.

Maybe she hadn't completely trusted Silas, but she would trust Colin to be the hero.

Still, maybe she could give him some help along the way. New determination filled her.

Buck squeezed her arm and jerked her forward then back. She glanced at him. He didn't know his way, after all. She didn't point out that he was lost. How could she use this?

She hadn't lived in Alaska without gaining a few skills, and on that point she had an advantage over Buck. Left lost and alone in the cave or even in the wilderness, he would be hard-pressed to survive.

But how did she get away from him, since he had a knife? If she could get her freedom and incapacitate him in some way, she could run back to Colin. Together they could escape.

Buck finally made his decision about which direction to traverse and dragged her down a tunnel to the right. Thankfully blue light filled the tunnel, lighting their path. But he'd made a bad choice. The walls closed in so that they had to slide through pressed against one side. Buck could only hold on to her arm with one hand. The knife was in his other hand.

Now.

Now was her chance. Likely the only good chance she would get. But it meant her plan to run back to Colin wouldn't work. Up ahead, the walls opened up more. Then her chance would be over.

Should she take this? Or wait for another one that she might not get?

Her temples throbbed. Time was running out. She had to make a decision. She had never been more indecisive in her life. But none of her options was good enough. There was no clear path to reach a good outcome.

"Keep moving." Buck's iron grip tightened. "What are you doing?"

Her hesitation had only made him grip harder. Why had she thought she could escape?

She kept moving forward. The wall of ice narrowed even more before it would open wider. Up ahead she spotted a jagged strip of ice protruding like a shard of broken glass. It would be tough to make it by without injury.

And *that*, she could use.

As she neared that sharp edge, Jewel took a few breaths, but failed to calm herself. What did it matter? She needed adrenaline flowing to make this happen.

Here it comes.

She inched forward, Buck gripping her arm.

Wait for it.

She pressed back and away as her body crossed over the ice knife.

Now.

She swallowed and pressed forward and against the wall just as Buck's hand gripping her arm followed. The jagged edge of the ice cut him quick and hard.

Behind her, he cried out.

His grip loosened only a little. It was enough.

Jewel broke free and pushed through the narrow passage until it widened. Then she ran. She didn't know where she was going, but she had to get away. In her mind she pictured Buck breaking free right behind her, but she knew his hand was badly mangled and the pain would slow him down.

From behind he shouted at her, using colorful language that singed her ears. But Jewel didn't look back. The problem was she could only move so fast through the ice cave without risking falling or slipping on icy patches.

With her breath rasping in her ears, she turned a corner. Paused and leaned against a wall. Listening for Buck.

Buck's ragged breaths echoed through the cave along with his angry rant. She couldn't let him catch her. He would kill her this time, diamond or no.

The cave angled down and deep.

No, no, no. She wanted an escape. But then she saw light ahead and heard a rushing, roaring sound. A familiar sound. A glacier stream forming a waterfall?

Jewel followed the sound and the light, running as fast as she could, knowing that Buck would be on her soon. The cave opened up over a partially frozen waterfall. The bottom churned with icy cold water as it rushed out into the open to connect with the river and then the channel.

The beauty took her breath away. But she had no time to appreciate it.

Buck was going to kill her if he caught up. *Lord, what do I do?*

If she jumped she would be free of Buck. Memories quickly seized her of her time fighting the other waterfall and then the rushing river. Surviving. Her body still ached. If she jumped her limbs would likely give up from the too-cold glacier water and she would drown.

Her choices came down to two.

Death by drowning.

Death by Buck.

Jewel wouldn't give him the satisfaction. Besides, she held on to hope that she could survive the icy water. It was more hope than she gave herself with Buck.

She lunged toward the falls.

Strong hands gripped her from behind.

* * *

Gun at the ready, Colin crept forward, following the voices.

The hardest thing he'd ever done in his life was to watch without interfering as Buck had forced Jewel away at knifepoint. Colin had decided it was better to bide his time again. Let the man believe Colin was too incapacitated to follow.

As soon as the two were out of sight and earshot, Colin had grabbed the extra magazine holding twelve bullets that he'd successfully hidden away and stuck it in the Sig, then chambered a round.

He had this one chance to get it right. To get Jewel away from Buck. He'd tried to make another call for help and explain the urgency, but had gotten no cell signal. He hadn't expected one, but had thought it was worth a shot.

And now as he followed the blood drops on the ground, his pulse ramped up. His heart pressed against his rib cage.

God, please don't let Jewel be hurt. Please help her, save her. Please help me to get there before it's too late this time. I can't go through losing someone again. I couldn't live with that. Jewel has to survive.

He heard the roaring of the falls before he turned the corner. Just up ahead, Buck's words were filled with hate and anger. This was the end of the line. One way or another, Buck was going down. Either Colin deserved to be an officer of the law, the chief of police, or he didn't. Regardless, Jewel deserved to live. She deserved his best effort.

Even his life.

Holding his weapon in position, Colin rounded the corner.

At the edge of the falls, Buck pulled Jewel's hair and yelled in her face. He flashed the knife in her face, letting her know what he wanted to do with her. Colin suspected he would follow through if it weren't for the diamond. All this couldn't be for nothing.

Still, Buck could kill Jewel even if Colin called out, threatening to shoot him.

Jewel cried out in pain as Buck twisted her hair around. She opened her eyes and saw Colin. Hope infused her face.

No, Jewel, don't telegraph that I'm here.

Colin's cell suddenly rang. He gripped the gun harder as Buck jerked around to face him. Stupid cell signals came through at the worst times. He ignored the call.

Jewel grabbed Buck's bloodied hand and jabbed her thumb into what Colin could see was a badly bleeding injury.

Buck threw her down, clearly not worried about her escape. She was between the waterfall and Buck. He could snatch her back before she jumped, if that had been her intention.

Colin closed the distance. Buck jerked up and around. Started for Jewel.

"Freeze!"

Buck moved to Jewel, grabbed her hair. Flashed the knife.

Colin fired at his feet. "I killed your brother. Don't think I won't kill you, too."

And Colin wanted to. God help him, he wanted to kill this man.

Buck dropped the knife. Did as he was told.

Colin ignored the voice screaming in his head, telling him to shoot the jerk. He had to do this right. Every decision he made had to be for the right reasons and not to seek vengeance for the past or for Jed's life. Or for Katelyn's.

God, I didn't know how hard it would be!

"Back away from her. Up against the wall."

Buck couldn't seem to lose his smirk, no matter what. Colin wanted to wipe it from his face. He tugged the handcuffs from his jacket pocket, offering a smile himself for thinking to bring them.

"You mean this whole time you carried those things with you?" Buck's eyes were round with shock.

Colin liked to see it. Liked to see he'd knocked the smirk from Buck's face, too.

"Guess you could say I was pretty confident this moment would come."

"The charges won't stick. You have nothing on me."

"I have Jewel's testimony."

"It's my word against hers."

"And mine."

"You're just trying to make up for the past. Your testimony won't count."

"Jewel, come over here away from the falls. Hold the weapon on Buck. Shoot him if he moves."

She moved toward Colin, relief shining in her eyes, and something more that made his heart swell. But he had to finish this business. Jewel took the weapon and aimed it at Buck. Her hands trembled as she slipped her finger into the trigger guard.

"Easy now," Colin said. "You don't want to shoot him accidentally."

Jewel nodded. Steadied her hand.

Colin approached Buck. "Hands out." They

still had to make their way out of here, so Buck would need his hands out in front.

"The charges will only stick if Jewel is around to give her testimony. You think she'll make it to trial? Don't you have enough experience to know better?"

Colin stared, the whole thing unfolding in his mind, reminiscent of the past. Close, much too close, to what had gone before. Buck and Brock had been working together, throwing the investigation.

"They'll stick because this time you're working alone." Colin cuffed one wrist.

An eerie look came into Buck's eyes. "I never work alone."

Colin cuffed the other. He had him this time. But the confidence he'd expected eluded him. Instead, he was more terrified for Jewel's life now that he knew what she'd face as a witness. Could he walk this path again?

And what had Buck said? He never worked alone?

This wasn't going to end. It was never going

to end until Buck was dead, too. Colin hesitated too long. Buck punched Colin in his already injured nose. Pain nearly blinded him. Colin gripped Buck, wrestling for control yet again, even though Buck was restrained in handcuffs.

He hoped Jewel wouldn't try to shoot, though he knew she could hit her target under normal circumstances. Buck slammed his fist into Colin's gunshot wound. Colin twisted Buck's injured hand, the battle roaring in his ears and growing louder.

Buck pushed Colin and he teetered on the lip of the cave, hovering over the ledge and waterfall. Just like before. And as he stared into Buck's cold, hard eyes, Colin knew without a doubt Buck had pushed him before, but had saved him in the end, just to be able to torment him a little longer.

What about now?

Colin flailed and reached out for his nemesis and gripped the short chain linking the cuffs, unsure if he meant to stop his own plunge or to take Buck Cambridge with him into the falls. Regardless of his intentions, a force beyond their control pulled them both down toward the frothing base of an icy waterfall.

Colin fell through empty space. Plunging fast. Buck released him. Time shifted. What took mere seconds seemed like minutes as they fell together. Jewel screamed his name from above, her cries melding with the rumble of the waterfall.

SIXTEEN

"No! Colin, *noooooooo!*"

The violent water rushed beneath the ice, then burst through halfway down the side of the cliff before churning at the base, drowning out her screams.

She watched the two men plummet, then disappear in mist and foam. Her heart sank beneath the water with them.

Oh, God. No.

How could he survive the drop to the bottom, much less the icy water? Fear wrapped around her very core. The day Silas had died she'd heard thunder, a rare event in this part of the world. She remembered thinking about that, but at that moment, she'd had no idea that the sound had followed the lightning strike that had killed Silas. Her husband.

And if she had been there to see it, what could she have done?

Nothing. Maybe she would have died with him.

But she couldn't stand here and do nothing now.

Jewel looked for a way to make it down from the cave. But it was a straight drop. Distress threatened to force her to her knees. She pushed down the panic and dread, turned and ran back through the cave, hoping she remembered the way out of the icy maze. She followed the drops of blood, easy enough to see on the white ice, then slipped through the thin walls where she'd made her escape. A lot of good that had done.

She was running, pushing herself harder, even though pain stitched her side. Jewel wasn't sure she could find her way back to the watercourse or what she could do to help Colin, but she had to try.

God, help him, help him, help him...

While she ran, she prayed harder than she'd

ever prayed. Whatever it meant, the deeper meaning of it, she didn't know or care. She only knew that Colin was everything to her. Finally, she could admit that now. Despite protecting her heart all these years, she was here all the same, losing someone she loved, if it wasn't already too late. But she wouldn't think like that. She couldn't lose him, too.

Finally, Jewel rushed from the cave's exit, then hurried back through the woods and around, taking the same direct path that Buck had forced her to go.

"Help!" she called as she ran. *God, please let there be someone out here to help me.* "Help me! Help us!"

She would have thought Colin would have called for backup once he'd discovered Buck had taken her. But maybe he hadn't had time before he'd come chasing after her. If so, then it was her fault for sneaking away. Maybe her mistake had been the catalyst to a tragic ending. Through the woods she could see the river in the distance. It spilled out from the falls a couple of miles from the visitor center. Out of breath, Jewel made her way to the riverbank, searching for Colin. Hoping she wouldn't see Buck.

"Colin!" she called, searching the water and rapids, remembering her own fight with a river.

Jewel only thought she had been helpless before.

She stumbled over a rock and fell to her knees at the river's edge.

And there.

Colin floated facedown in the water. Dread washed through her. Jewel stepped into the liquid ice and hauled him onto the bank. He was heavy, especially with wet clothing, but Jewel was undeterred. Jewel tugged him up farther away from the bank, then rolled him over to immediately start CPR.

She could only hope and pray he hadn't been in this condition for long—five minutes or less and the freezing glacier water would slow any neurological effects like brain damage.

Colin rolled to the side and coughed. Then he got to all fours, hung his head and expelled the river that had nearly drowned him. Groaning, he fell back on his back. His eyes cut to Jewel, but he said nothing.

What was he thinking? "Your lips are blue," she said, breaking the silence between them. "We have to get you warmed up."

"Jewel." He lifted a hand. She leaned in to let him cup her cheek. "You saved me."

"You're the real hero here, Colin. You saved me first. Protected me, then rescued me from Buck. If you hadn't been there…"

His gaze clouded over, a flicker of emotion shuttered away. What was Colin thinking? Did he hold her responsible? This all had come about because of her mistake. Colin had almost lost his life because of her. And he still might if they didn't get him warmed up.

Shivering, Colin twisted and climbed to his feet. Jewel joined him. He started to pull her into his arms and then hesitated. Because of his disappointment in her?

"For whatever it's worth," she said, "I'm sorry about everything."

"Oh, Jewel." Again, he cupped her cheek. His hand was as cold as ice. "No need to apologize. I just…I don't want to make you any colder."

He shook almost uncontrollably and blood oozed from the bloodshot wound. Not good. Blood loss was dangerous enough on its own—it was worse when he was struggling against hypothermia. Jewel wrapped her arms around him. She could use her body heat to warm him until help arrived. Was help even coming? "Does anyone know where we are?"

"I called for help when I learned he had taken you."

"It's taking them long enough."

He nodded. "There."

Jewel let go of him to see where he pointed. Coughing, he stumbled forward. Jewel couldn't hold him up without following him.

In the distance she spotted two men hiking toward them.

"Looks like someone from the state police and the local PD," Colin said. "We still need to find Buck."

The two men approached. Jewel spoke first. "We need to get him somewhere warm. I pulled him from the river." She explained as best she could everything that happened and that Colin had helped her to escape a kidnapper.

"Thank you, ma'am. We'll take it from here," the state trooper said.

"The kidnapper might still be in the river," Colin said. "We need a search and rescue."

One officer nodded and assisted Colin up and took him away. The other got on his radio to get a SAR mission number initiated.

Jewel followed, worried the hike down would take too long. Colin had called for help, for backup in taking Buck in, but not for medical assistance.

Hiking behind them she listened as Colin

explained about Buck. That he could be dead or he could have escaped.

Oh, Meral! How would Jewel tell her sister? She would be devastated. After their argument, Meral could still believe Buck was innocent, and the blame for this would fall on Jewel.

Then she remembered Buck's words. *I never work alone.*

A chill ran over her, adding to the cold that had seeped into her bones. She glanced at the woods around them as they hiked. Was someone out there watching?

This wasn't over yet.

Colin sat in the park ranger's office off the glacier visitor center, wrapped in a blanket and drinking hot coffee. Considering that he had nearly drowned, he thought he was past the worst of it. He'd let the ranger use the GSW kit on his superficial wound until he could get real medical attention.

No time for that yet.

The trooper stepped into the room. "We found a body that matches your description. His hands were cuffed. He seems to have drowned."

Colin hung his head. "He never had a chance."

Jewel entered the small room, her eyes red rimmed. The fierce need to comfort and protect her rose up in him. Why had he ever denied himself loving this woman? The battle with Buck and then the waterfall had opened his eyes. Losing his life until she had revived him, the excuses he'd made before seemed just that. Excuses. But…she was a wealthy woman far out of his league. Colin had been out of his league before with Katelyn, and it hadn't ended well. He would do what was best and walk away from anything more with Jewel. They were not finished with this business, and Colin needed to keep his head in the game.

"We need to tell Meral. How are we going to tell her?" Jewel asked.

The authorities were trying to locate *The Alabaster Sky*, which had pulled anchor and disappeared.

Colin had already given his statement, as had Jewel, but there was one thing he'd forgotten. He stood and let the blanket drop. "Cambridge said he didn't work alone."

Silence filled the small office as the words sank in. The ranger sitting across from him scratched his chin.

"But that doesn't mean it was Meral," Jewel pleaded. "When he first captured me, he said he had drugged her. That she had slept through all the incidents. That she was clueless. She isn't his partner."

No. Just his wife.

"Regardless, we need to tell her what's happened to her husband." Colin eyed Jewel. Telling someone they had lost a loved one was the worst part of being a police officer. "And maybe we can find out the truth, including the identities of Buck's accomplice or accomplices. But you need to stay vigilant, Jewel. Your life could still be in danger."

And he knew that well enough from his past.

Ryan, the police officer who assisted Colin, rushed back into the office. "We've located *The Alabaster Sky* docked at Alder's Bay." He nodded at Jewel and Colin. "I'll transport you there."

"Wait," Colin said.

"What are you thinking?" Jewel asked.

"The yacht has to be waiting to rendezvous with Buck. I hadn't suspected the crew, but now I don't know if the crew or the captain is involved in his crimes or not. This could be our chance to find out."

"Buck planned to take me back so I could show him where I'd hid the diamond. Other than tearing the boat apart, I don't know how he would have found it."

"What's your plan?" Ryan asked.

"I'll return to the yacht and gather the staff and Meral and tell them what's happened,"

Colin said. "We'll see how they react. If you wouldn't mind sticking around, maybe you can catch anyone who tries to leave. In the meantime, can you get someone to run a background on the crew of *The Alabaster Sky*? See who might have any connection to Buck Cambridge."

"I'm going, too," Jewel said. "This is my sister. I want to be there for her."

Colin hung his head, wondering if Jewel would ever forgive him for his next words. "I'm not sure that's a good idea, Jewel. Despite what you believe, Meral could still be party to Buck's crimes."

Her eyes blazed. "Look. I know my sister, okay? She isn't capable of this."

He didn't have the heart to remind her that she hadn't known her sister for at least the past twenty years of her life. "I hope you're right, Jewel. For your sake, I hope you're right. But we can't ignore that possibility, and in that case, you're vulnerable. She could threaten your life to save her own."

His words cut her. He could see it in her eyes, but they had to be said.

With a deep frown in her brow, she rubbed her arms and averted her gaze. But she said nothing in response. She knew it was true.

With his words he'd begun to sever his emotional connection to Jewel. He could see it in her eyes. Nearly losing himself, everything that had happened, had him vulnerable and willing to let himself love. But he'd come to his senses. He couldn't let himself get any closer.

Caring too much for Jewel had kept him from pressing for answers from the start. If he had just pushed harder, found out about the diamond earlier, then maybe Buck would be in jail instead of dead, and Jed would still be alive. Getting emotionally involved just caused problems.

Back in Texas he was too close to the witness in a case, and he'd kept that under wraps because his chief would have taken the case from him. But he'd fallen in love with her and had wanted to be close and keep his hands on the investigation. To make sure things were done right and she was safe, he'd told himself. And all along, he'd had his eyes on the wrong man.

That had cost her her life.

A person could never know where seemingly innocent decisions would lead or what lives would be affected. Knowing was beyond the realm of humanity. Only God knew these things.

What irony that his bringing charges against the wrong man over a decade ago in Texas would end in him facing off with the right man years later. Colin feared his own mistakes—both from the past and more recently—would cost Jewel more than her diamond.

He couldn't trust himself to protect her. He couldn't rely on his own strength. He'd done that before and had failed.

Please, God, help me to keep her safe!

SEVENTEEN

Jewel boarded *The Alabaster Sky* with Colin, her heart torn over what she was about to do. She had successfully negotiated that she would be the one to tell Meral. But Colin wanted the staff there to hear the news at the same time and went to find them all. Jewel didn't like this.

There had to be a better way to find Buck's partner in crime.

She found Meral in the salon, curled up with a blanket around her. Worry lines made her look much older. Jewel rushed to her. Meral immediately jumped up and hugged her sister.

"You're back. I thought you weren't coming." Meral held Jewel at arm's length and then, seeming to remember their earlier argument, dropped her arms. "What's happened? Why are you back?"

Meral's gaze reflected her fear of the worst. She moved away from Jewel and continued. "Tell me what's going on."

Jewel opened her mouth, but she couldn't find the words. Where did she start? But Meral started jabbering instead.

"After everything that happened, I had a headache and took a nap. Buck's so good to me. He found my pills to help me rest. When I woke up, he was gone. Stella told me he would be back soon, but she didn't say where he'd gone. He isn't answering his phone. For all the good cells do around here. But that doesn't explain why you're here, Jewel." Meral's eyes softened. "Unless you've come to apologize. That's it, isn't it? I hope you know how wrong you were about Buck and you're going to stay now."

The way Meral rambled on, Jewel could see how someone else might suspect her of being guilty of knowing something, but from Jewel's perspective, it was clear she'd been sleeping. Her speech was even slightly slurred. Buck had told the truth on that point. He had drugged her.

"Meral." Colin stepped in.

Behind him stood the other crew members he'd gathered together.

Jewel had intended to break the harsh news, but she lost her nerve. She stepped back, standing next to him, giving him permission, though he needed none. Even though he had taken a bullet and had almost drowned, strength and confidence emanated from him. Jewel tried to soak it in. She was going to need strength to help Meral.

"I'm sorry to have to tell you that your husband is gone."

Meral gasped. "Gone? What do you mean?"

"I'm sorry, but he was found dead."

They had made a mistake by being the ones to do this. Now Meral would want to know how it had happened. How would she react when she learned both Jewel and Colin were involved? She might blame them. Accuse them.

Glass shattered behind them.

Glancing back, Stella's face contorted. She covered her mouth. She looked at Colin. Must have seen something in his eyes. Recognition? She turned and ran up the steps to the deck.

Colin gave Jewel a glance and took off after her. Jewel should stay with her sister, but she feared for Colin, too. If Stella was Buck's partner, then she must be the one who had forced Jewel's Durango off the road. That meant she was as dangerous as Buck was.

Jewel ran up the steps and onto the deck, but didn't see Colin or Stella.

Where had they gone? Had Stella jumped overboard and Colin followed her? Jewel rushed to the rail and looked over into the water.

Nothing.

Eerie tingles ran over her arm. "Colin," she whispered. "Where are you?"

This wasn't how any of this was supposed to happen. What about Colin's backup near the dock, waiting to corral anyone who tried to escape?

Jewel realized her foolishness. She would go back down with Meral and wait this out. But she felt cold plastic against her head. A Glock? How many times would she go through this?

"You're coming with me," Stella said.

"Why are you doing this?"

"You killed my father."

"Buck is your *father*?"

"Yes. Dad and I worked together. This should have been an easy job, but you just wouldn't give up."

"You mean I just wouldn't die."

"Your words. Not mine. Now tell me where you hid the diamond. I can't leave here without something to show for it. I need something from you to make up for my loss. It's either that or your life."

All this time, Stella must have been searching, even while Buck had kidnapped Jewel, and she still hadn't found the diamond on the yacht. Jewel had to keep her talking until Colin could find them.

"How did you get a job on this yacht? Or is the whole crew involved?"

Stella scoffed, digging the gun deeper. "Because that's how it all played out. I got the job when the other steward conveniently became ill. Dad convinced the other guests who'd already booked the boat to take a later cruise. He paid them for their time. Who could say no to that? Dad's brilliant. He knows how to work things. Or at least he did."

"Where's Colin? What did you do to him?"

"Shh." Stella tugged her back into the shadows. "Say one word and I'll kill him."

Colin jogged around the deck, clearly looking for Stella.

Stella tugged her deeper into the shadows. Pulling Jewel closer, Stella shifted the gun and pressed it into Jewel's side, sending her message loud and clear. Like father like daughter.

Enough of this.

Even with the gun pressed in her side, Jewel knew she could take Stella. She was beyond tired of this, and it would never end until Jewel ended it.

She used the same moved she'd used in the attic on Buck, slamming her head back. It worked beautifully and left Stella splayed on the deck, gun sliding away.

And then Colin was there, standing slack mouthed and staring at Stella. He looked from her up to Jewel and grinned.

"Finally." Jewel dusted off her hands. "Meet Buck's daughter and partner in crime."

Colin radioed to the other officers, who quickly boarded the yacht and took Stella into custody. Jewel went back into the salon to find Meral curled in a ball, sobbing. It would take her time to accept all that had happened.

* * *

Back at the B and B, Meral and Jewel tried to come to grips with everything they'd been through during the past few days. Statements had been given, the Krizan Diamond referred to as a family heirloom. Meral explained it had never been reported missing or stolen, convincing Jewel that it belonged to her as much as anyone in the family. Jewel wasn't sure what to do or how to feel about that.

With everyone questioned, finally the investigation was closed. Stella had been arrested and charged as an accomplice to murder, plus attempted murder and numerous other crimes involving jewel theft throughout the country.

But that didn't mean it was over. Not for Meral, whose life as she knew it was ruined.

"I'm so sorry, honey." Jewel ran her hand over Meral's head, hoping to comfort her, but there could be no comfort for Meral. Only time would bring healing. Jewel was glad Meral would stay with her for the time being.

"How could he do this to me? I thought he loved me. I don't understand." Meral sobbed into another tissue and shook her head. The pain in her eyes broke Jewel's heart. She couldn't help but feel that in a way—a long, roundabout way—she'd done this to her sister.

"How can I ever trust again? How can I ever love again?" Meral asked.

Jewel had thought she would never trust or love again herself after losing Silas, so she understood Meral's misgivings. "First you have to heal and you need to give yourself time. I once thought I could never love again. But now I realize I was just scared. Trusting is a risk, yes. Loving again is a risk. Then I found someone special, and now I'm willing to take that risk."

Meral blinked up at her. "Chief Winters."

"Colin. I'm in love with him. I tried to deny it, to hide it, to keep it from surfacing, but what is life without love?" Jewel regretted her words. This wasn't the time. "I'm sorry, Meral. I shouldn't have..."

"No, it's okay. I think...deep down, I knew something was going on with Buck. That his business wasn't on the up-and-up. I didn't understand it anyway, so I just chose to look the other way. If anything, I should be the one who is sorry. If it wasn't for me, he never would have come after you."

"No. You have nothing to apologize for. Wait here. I have something to show you." While they'd dined on the deck that first night, Jewel had left to quickly refresh herself in her cabin, and she'd taken that chance to transfer the diamond to Meral's luggage, where no one would think to look. Jewel tugged open Meral's luggage now and rummaged around until she found the inner lining. From there she pulled out the Krizan Diamond and held it out to Meral. "I want you to have this. I don't want it. I don't want to be wealthy. I don't want or need anything except, well maybe..."

"Your police chief."

"Right, except I'm not sure he'll have me now that he knows I stole a diamond. That I'm kind of a jewel thief like the man who killed the woman he loved years ago. To have a chance with him, I think he needs to know I no longer have the diamond. I'm giving it up. He needs to know that I trust him. I didn't trust Silas, not enough, but somehow I have to convince Colin that I trust him enough not to need a backup plan anymore. I have to convince him to forgive me for not telling him everything when it mattered the most. When it could have made a difference."

Meral eyed the precious gem. "I don't want it, Jewel. I can't take it. It will only remind me of Buck's duplicity. You keep it." Meral curled back into a ball.

Jewel held on to it, wanting nothing more than to throw it into the ocean. She hung her head, wishing she could get back the past few days. If she could, she would do everything differently. She would tell Colin everything, maybe even that she loved him.

Someone cleared a throat.

Jewel looked up. Colin. He gestured that he wanted to speak with her. Meral was resting with her eyes closed. Jewel left her sister, who needed privacy, time alone anyway. Meral needed some space to process the pain. It would take years for it to go away completely, but now that she had fully faced the truth, she could start the healing process.

Heart beating unevenly, Jewel approached Colin and held out the diamond for him to see. "How long have you been standing there?"

Had he heard her confession of love?

He tipped her chin up. "Long enough."

Her gaze widened slightly. He saw uncertainty there as he drank deeply from the pool of her hazel-green eyes. He touched the soft skin of her cheek, twisted his finger in a tendril of her ash-blond hair.

She held the diamond out, and it shimmered in the dim light. He'd been so busy with everything there hadn't been time to see the "family heirloom" that had caused the trouble.

The yellow stone glistened and sparkled and took his breath away. Never had he seen anything like it up close and personal.

Jewel began explaining about cut, color and clarity. "It's just over twenty carats, natural fancy intense and internally flawless."

"If you say so," he said. All the diamond-speak had his head spinning.

"Do you know they have to mine over two hundred and fifty tons of ore just to find a one-carat colored diamond? And the radiant cut means it has seventy-seven facets."

Colin wouldn't tell her he had no idea what she was talking about. How could he when she was clearly in her element? The diamond looked like she'd captured sunshine in the palm of her hand, and that sunshine reflected on her face as she talked about what was near and dear to her heart—her family and the family diamond business. She may have left it all behind twenty years earlier, but she clearly hadn't forgotten a thing.

The fact she talked long and knowledgeable on a subject he knew absolutely nothing about reminded him all too well she was out of his league, really, as he'd always thought.

He pressed a finger on it—cold to the touch—and sucked in a breath.

And then he knew he couldn't do it. He couldn't step away from her. This diamond might be cold, but the jewel before him was anything but.

He wrapped her hand around the diamond and covered it with his own. "This isn't the jewel I want. This belongs to you. Your confession, your past, has no bearing on how I feel about you, Jewel Caraway. How I've always felt but denied."

His throat grew tight. "I thought that you and I would both be better off if I stepped back. Turned away from this force that pulls me to you at every turn, but I'm not strong enough to walk away from you anymore. You're more precious to me than anything in this world. Even my own life. And I've wasted so much time already."

He searched her eyes for understanding. For the love he wanted to see reflected in her gentle hazel gaze, unclouded by fear or uncertainty or doubt. And he was not disappointed.

How many years had he imagined, dreamed about this moment, then shoved aside his longing to do what he had thought was right for them both? But right now he was weak, so very weak. His will bowed to the current running between them, a quaking force that shook him to the bones. Or maybe he was finally strong enough to accept the path that God had wanted for him all along. To stop running in fear from the prospect of getting hurt again.

Colin slowly wrapped his arms around Jewel and pressed his lips against hers. She kissed him back, and he savored her response.

Accepting. Eager.

Ecstasy. He was enraptured at the slightest pressure of her soft lips. Any more and he would lose himself completely. He breathed in deeply the jewel he'd longed for, and realized that somehow his heart had carved the perfect place for her within him.

He could have stayed forever with Jewel in his arms, letting her know how he felt about her, but he had to rein in his emotions. It was dangerous to linger. He inched back. Still, he was close to her, closer than he'd ever been physically and emotionally, even spiritually. There was something about loving a woman who loved God, and he could feel that in her, as well.

He let go of his resolve never to love. God didn't want that for him, and he didn't want it for himself—not when he had the treasure of Jewel's love as recompense. Her heart in exchange for his own.

"I heard you tell Meral that you loved me. I love you, too, Jewel. I think I always have."

Her eyes shimmered with what he hoped were tears of joy along with her beautiful smile. Despite the tragedy and pain around them, she was free of her stalker and her past, as was Colin.

"This experience has taught me something," he said.

"What's that?" Her voice was lyrical, and he loved that about it.

It felt wonderful to be free finally to enjoy everything about Jewel, instead of always pushing thoughts of her away.

"If I didn't know before, I know now how precious life is and I don't want to waste a single moment. I don't want to waste time regretting the past or fearing the future. I don't need days, weeks or months to get to know you. I've known you for years. I'll court you, ask you on a real date first, if that's what you want, but I feel like in my heart I've been secretly courting you for years. And there's so much more I want to do with you."

She laughed and nodded, wiped at a tear.

"Will you be my wife, Jewel? Will you marry me?"

She shuddered, hung her head back, but the look on her face was pure elation. Then she rolled her head forward and smiled. "How about next week? You can marry me first, and I'll take the courting for a lifetime."

* * * * *

Dear Reader,

Thank you so much for reading *Deception*. I hope you enjoyed the story as much as I enjoyed writing it. Though I can't relate to coming from an old-money family or even being part of a family diamond business, I can relate to making mistakes in the past that I still regret to this day. What about you? Have you ever made a simple decision that turned out to be a mistake with far-reaching repercussions? If you're human, of course you have. We all have. We often carry the weight of that mistake around like a heavy burden that affects other decisions, as well.

If only we could know the future, there are probably many decisions we would have made differently. Though we can't know what will happen, the good news is that we can trust God for our future, and we can also trust Him to take care of our past. Sometimes there are still repercussions, but those are easier to bear when we give the burden over to God and accept His grace.

I love this scripture: *As far as the east is from the west, so far has he removed our transgressions from us*, Psalm 103:12, and often meditate on it to remind me that I am forgiven as far as God is concerned—and He is the only One who really matters. He is the One we answer to.

I hope and pray you found a nugget of truth in the story, even as you enjoyed the ride. I love to hear from my readers, so please be sure to visit my website at http://elizabethgoddard.com to find out how to connect with me and to sign up for my newsletter to receive book news and updates.

Many blessings!
Elizabeth Goddard